BITE ME

A DRAGONS LOVE CURVES NOVEL

AIDY AWARD

Aidy Award/Coffee Break Publishing

www.coffeebreakpublishing.com

Publisher's Note: This is a work of fiction. Names, characters, places, and incidents are a product of the author's imagination. Locales and public names are sometimes used for atmospheric purposes. Any resemblance to actual people, living or dead, or to businesses, companies, events, institutions, or locales is completely coincidental.

Cover by Melody Simmons

Bite Me/ Aidy Award. — 1st ed.

ASIN B07D4FHC63

ISBN 978-0-9904060-6-8

SHE'S STOLEN A SOUL... AND HIS HEART.

Ky Puru is the best chance anyone has to get the soul of the Golden Dragon Wyvern back. Nothing will stand in his way - not demons, not witches, not even the king of hell himself. There's only one problem. Jada, the thief, is a succubus...and his true mate.

Jada needs to get away from her coven and find a life she can call her own. If it involves baked goods instead of blood, that would be great. But, that's not going to happen, and this sexy dragon warrior that wants to claim her as his mate is the reason why.

Neither Ky nor Jada ever thought they would have a true mate, and they may not get that chance when an evil foe attacks and will do everything he can to make sure no dragon ever gets to find their fated mate or fall in love.

This dragon alpha and his curvy succubus mate will have go to hell and back, literally, for their chance at their own happy ever after.

For Diana, my very best Kiwi

E tama, te uaua ana
E tama, te mārō
Roa ina hoki ra
Te tohe o te uaua na
E tāu nei.
Āna! Āna! Āna! Aue... Hī!

So son, although it may be difficult for you
and son, although it seems to be unyielding
no matter how long you reflect on it
the answer to the problem
is here inside you.
Indeed! Indeed! Indeed! Yes, indeed!

—The Māori *Tika Tonu* Haka

TOO MANY DEMONS, NOT ENOUGH DONUTS

*T*oo many demons in the kitchen spoils the soup. Or in this case donuts.

A batch of carbtastic sugary bombs of deliciousness sizzled away in the fryer, while Jada dreamed of all the decadent toppings she would put on them.

Chocolate frosting, check.

Maple cream, check.

Rainbow sprinkles. Ew, gross.

Toffee chunks. Yep.

Caramel drizzle, double check.

Some B positive, AB neg, or how about some good ol' O universal? Hells to the no.

That's what Leon wanted. It was what he always wanted. But, not only for himself. For her too.

Her father shouldn't be in the kitchen of the summer rental harassing her anyway. He didn't even like sugar or cooking or kitchens. He didn't like anything but sex and blood.

The scent of vanilla and cinnamon wafted through the air

and smelled almost as good as the humans Jada waiting in the great room.

The rest of her coven was already playing with their prey. Seducing and taunting, testing and tasting, picking out the right one to satisfy their darkest urges.

The men and women Leon had lured to the ocean-side mansion were wanting and willing. A night of sexual carousing with the most sensual summer residents of the Cape was enough to tempt these unsuspecting humans to their doom. That and Leon's hypnotic incubus allure.

Jada smelled their growing arousal already. Its dark, rich, deliciousness sang to her core.

Her heart jumped, racing to catch up with the others.

A pulsing beat pushed between her legs.

Her mouth watered.

She wanted to sink her teeth into… a donut. Pure chocolate glaze running down her throat, hot and sweet. She'd take the sugar high over blood lust all day, every day, twice on Sundays.

It was the little lies she told herself that got her through the days and long, long nights.

"Jada, why do you waste your time on these human treats when there are so many delicious humans to be our treats?"

God damn it. A few more minutes and the most perfect batch of her yumtastic feast would be ready. "Go away, Leon."

He propped himself against the kitchen island and crossed his arms. "Now, now, is that any way to talk to your maker?"

As if he cared how she spoke to him. He only cared that her absence from the nightly orgies was sowing discontent amongst the coven.

He could take his fatherly disapproval and shove it up his donut hole.

"I'm not going to your Bacchanalia. Not tonight, not ever again. I'm done with human blood."

"Yes, yes. You say that every few years." He cracked his knuckles one by one. "And are you done with the pleasures their flesh brings you too?

Sex.

She'd had enough of it to last most succubae a lifetime, or two, and she was only half demon. But, she wanted more, all the time. Sex was going to be a hell of a lot harder to give up than the blood.

The kitchen timer dinged, and Jada ignored Leon's question in favor of flipping over each of the half dozen beautifully browning cake donuts, revealing their perfectly fried underbellies. As soon as they cooled, she would smother them in rich chocolate ganache and sprinkle with chocolate chip cookie crumbles.

Three of those and a glass of milk to dunk them in were better than sex.

Almost.

"You can ignore me, fruit of my loins, but you cannot deny your true nature."

"Ehhhh." She made a sound like the buzzer in a Q&A game. "I can, and I will. Thanks for playing. Bu-bye now."

She flipped him the bird and turned to the refrigerator. He was getting to her and he knew it.

So what if she'd tried to give up human blood before? This time she had a better plan.

Replace sex with food. Replace blood with… well she hadn't figured that part out yet.

No way she waiting long enough to glaze the donuts. Chocolate milk would have to cool them off. She'd risk burning her tongue, the roof of her mouth, and her esophagus.

"If you won't come to my little party, I'll simply have to bring it to you."

The bastard wouldn't.

She ripped open the fridge door and accidentally crushed the carton of milk in her fist.

"Come in, young man. I want you to meet my daughter."

Oh hell. Leon's allure had every spark of arousal firing out of this victim. It wrapped around her and slipped into her mouth and nose. The prey was horny and hard already.

That pulsing between her legs picked up a new faster, deeper rhythm. A shiver snaked across her chest and shoulders.

Her fingers dug into the milk container and the liquid dripped down her hand. She was not beneath licking chocolate milk off her arm. Anything to quash the mouthwatering scent of the human man standing behind her.

"Let me help you with that, luscious vampire mistress." The guy's deep voice seeped into her ears. He took her wrist in his hand and pulled it back, raising it to his mouth. The second his lips touched her, a zing of pure need rushed through Jada, hitting her right behind the heart. Her fangs extended, ready to taste his pleasure.

Pleasure and pain. What this guy offered her was both.

She wanted him.

She needed him.

Even more than sugar, sweets, or even breathing. He would take her body, not understanding that she was taking his life. The sex would be phenomenal, and then he would die.

Because Jada couldn't control herself. She would make

him come, sucking up his sexual energy and then she'd drink his blood until there was only a husk of the man left.

He would taste better than Dunkin, Krispy, Horton's, and Voodoo combined. The essence of his life would re-energize her, renew her, make her whole again.

Jada was so, so empty.

She'd tried for weeks to fill the gaping black hole inside of her with every comfort food the restaurants on the Cape could deliver to her. She'd tried for years to ignore the wounds her very existence continually slashed on her soul.

The only thing that came even close to the high sex and blood gave her was mounds of sugar.

She understood how millions of Americans were literally addicted to the stuff. It lit up all the right parts in the mortal half of her brain.

Not in the same way as the aroused naked man licking his way up her arm.

Maybe just one taste.

She'd be able to stop this time.

Only a little blood. If she kept the emotions buried, the human part of her that came with sex, she'd be able to control herself, only take what she needed, less if she really concentrated.

Jada let the guy kiss her shoulder, then her neck. His cock was pressed into her side, hard and ready for so much more. Lust and need poured out of him.

It was seductive, delicious.

No, blood only.

No sex.

No emotion.

It was the only way to control herself. Leon had been trying to teach her that for years.

She turned in the man's arms and he pushed her up against the refrigerator. She didn't even mind the handle jabbing her in the back. That didn't matter. Only the sexual energy pouring out of him and into her.

The scent of his carnal nature taking over was overwhelming her.

No. She wouldn't take any of it from him.

Not tonight. Not ever again. She wouldn't allow it.

"You vampires like it rough, don't you?" He shoved her hands up over her head and bit at her neck, pretending to be something he wasn't.

Another foolish human, falling prey to the legend of the vampire, not understanding the truth behind it.

Thousands of years of demons. Exactly like her.

The sting of his teeth and the way he sucked at her flesh was far from the violence she'd do to him. But, not before he got his rocks off. That made the blood, the energy, the kill so much sweeter.

Jada shifted her hips and wrapped one leg around his waist. He was so ready to go that she didn't even need her own hypnotic allure. He took her bait and began thrusting against her, dry humping her like he was made for it.

How she wanted to strip her yoga pants off and shove his hands, his mouth, and his cock between her legs.

She turned her head to the side and closed her eyes, pushing away any thought of her own pleasure. This had to be enough. This was the only way she could keep it together, keep him safe.

The rest of the humans were likely already dead. Sucked and fucked to death.

Murdered by the demon hunger.

A couple of deep breaths and she was able to open her eyes

again. That was a mistake. It put Leon into her line of sight. Disgusting.

His chin was tipped up and he breathed the sexual energy in from across the room.

Didn't matter that he was her father, that it was ten-levels-of-hell wrong to be watching her and this man together. None of that meant shit to him. All Leon cared about was siphoning the lust pouring off the man as he humped her leg. That's what an Incubus King did.

Enough.

Jada yanked her hands from the man's grasp and grabbed his head. Saliva dripped from her fangs. She pushed his head sideways and scraped her teeth across the artery in his neck. The blood vibrated under his skin, calling to her.

He groaned and lost his rhythm, thrusting at her frantically. "Yeah, baby. I'm close. Bite me. I'm gonna come."

She already tasted the edge of his orgasm, hot like the most intense spices. She wanted more.

The evil inside of her needed more.

Jada sunk her teeth into his neck and sucked the first drops of blood down like the finest wine.

"Fuck, oh, fuck. I'm coming. Ahhh."

The spicy flavor of his blood and orgasm shot into her cells. She went from sipping to gulping. Taking everything she could from him.

"Yes, Jada. Take him. He is so delectable." Leon crooned his own gratification.

He was more than delectable. He was life.

The man's head lolled to the side, and still she drank. She wasn't yet satisfied. He could give her more.

A squawking beep beep beep jumped into the room, invading her consciousness, making her cringe at its assault of her ears. Wisps of acrid smoke circled the air and the scent of burned sugar permeated the room.

The donuts. She'd forgotten the donuts.

Thank god.

She pulled her teeth from the neck of the man, and he slumped in her arms.

"Hey, hey. Buddy, uh, dude." Shit, she didn't even know his name. She slapped his cheek, trying to rouse him. He fell to the floor in a giant heap.

The muscles in Jada's chest contracted, pulling tight around her heart.

No, no, no. She'd killed him. Killed another one.

Fuck. She should have known better. She'd never been able to control herself before. What made her think she would be able to stop this time? Donuts?

They might be manna from heaven, but she was from hell.

The man at her feet groaned.

Holy shit. He was still alive.

Jada dropped to the floor and patted his chest. His skin was clammy and much too pale. "Hey, guy, hey, wake up."

"Don't be stupid, Jada. It's too late. Finish him." Leon towered over her. His skin was flushed, in so much contrast to the man near death.

Leon stretched his arms wide and smiled like he'd woken from a long-needed nap. He'd enjoyed every minute of the act that made Jada now feel sick to her stomach.

Deeper than that. She felt sick to her soul.

She couldn't do this, couldn't keep on killing. It wasn't right. She wasn't right.

The revulsion bubbled up, burning the back of her throat, until she couldn't hold it in any longer. She bolted to the sink and hurled into it.

Red blood splashed against the shiny steel.

Never again.

"Why do you insist on torturing yourself? This is who you are, little girl. This is what you are. Why are you always fighting it? After all these years, I'm growing tired of your antics."

Three hundred years. Countless lives lost so that she could live.

There had to be something more out there. In the past few months, a change worked inside of her, tugging at her psyche, pushing away the banal existence she led. It made her want that something more from life, more than death.

The empty pit in her stomach widened. She could never have whatever it was.

Without responding to Leon, she rinsed the blood down the drain and walked to the kitchen door.

"Leave now, and the life you spared will be no more." Her father's tone darkened, the demon snarl dominating his statement.

If she left, Leon would kill the man. If she stayed, Leon would kill her. Not directly, not by force, but by an eternity of his twisted form of preservation.

Jada saw that now. She would never be able to resist the call of sex and blood, and Leon would never let her.

Pure demon was what he was. No emotion, no compunction about killing innocent humans he lured to their deaths.

Taking more lives would kill her, but so would not taking them. At least if she left, she could make the choice of who and when and maybe how much.

If she couldn't leave, there was one last life she could take and end it all.

Being half human had to have some advantage.

Guilt clawed at her for leaving the guy to the mercy of Leon and her brothers and sisters. She would regret not getting away from the coven even more so.

She'd gotten as far as the kitchen door. Now, all she had to do was walk through it and out of this way of life. But, she was afraid. Without a coven, without Leon she would have no one. A succubus on her own was a dead succubus.

Dead inside or dead.

She took one step.

"I'm talking to you."

She didn't care or she didn't want to Not anymore.

"You walk away from me, and I won't be able to protect you." Leon's voice was somewhere in between pissed and concerned.

She kept going into the hallway, and up the stairs. Leon followed her all the way to her bedroom door. She tried to slam it in his face, but he caught it.

"I don't need your protection. I'm a big girl vampire now." She said the taunt in her best snotty little kid voice. Leon loved to play into the façade humans had invented to explain their kind.

"You have no idea, Jada."

Nice threat. She folded her arms and rolled her eyes at him. He always hated that. She was the only one of his offspring who wasn't in awe of him, who didn't think he hung the moon. It was one of the only things she still liked about herself.

He grinned, the evil inside making him look more creepy than happy. "You're being hunted."

Haunted was more like it. She tapped her foot. The more she annoyed him, the sooner he'd leave her alone.

"Demon dragons have attacked our coven a dozen times

over the past few months, and we've kept you in the dark about it, and thus safe."

Demon dragons. After her. "What are you talking about?"

Demons didn't attack each other. Each faction was focused on what they needed from humans. They had enemies of their own to worry about. Hunters tried to destroy the children of Lilith and dragons warriors kept the Black Dragon's plague at bay.

Leon studied her face and pushed at her consciousness to see if her reaction to his news was genuine. "What is bringing this resurgence in your reluctance to connect with the coven?"

Jada shifted from one foot to the other. This was an old fight between the two of them. Leon never got why she wasn't like the others.

He narrowed his eyes. "I sent Portia to the continent to keep her from telling you about the demon dragons. May she finally learn her lesson about being loyal to coven and not the individual."

Jada wished she had that same ability to know when someone wasn't telling her the truth. She'd inherited a lot of Leon's abilities, but that wasn't one of them. She'd have to guess. "You're lying to keep me here."

"I'm not. Ask your sister when she returns. She's fought off more of the beasts than anyone else. Leave this house and risk your life."

Jada's life wasn't worth much anyway. Maybe death by demon dragon was the way to go. Her only regret was leaving Portia behind. She was the only other person in the coven who ever understood.

Hopefully, her sister would understand her decision to leave too.

"I think I will."

Leon shrugged. "Fine. I'll be here when you need to come crying back to daddy."

Ew.

Jada shoved some of her favorite clothes into a bag, grabbed the money she'd been hoarding to buy human food, and searched around until she found the courage she'd been lacking for hundreds of years.

Succubae didn't survive on their own. That's why they formed covens under the succubus or incubus who created them.

The fastest way to kill a succubus wasn't a stake through the heart, or daylight, or garlic, like in the misinformed legends. It was banishment.

She'd basically banished herself.

Hell's big sweaty balls.

Jada hit the street running. Okay, not actually running. That would require moving her muscles more than her jiggly butt was capable of doing. Too many donuts. She did hurry along though.

Without a coven, she had no place to stay, no place to eat.

Except the donut shop out by the golf course but, it didn't open for a few more hours. Like eight.

It would take half that long to walk there anyway.

"Hey, baby. Where you going? Need a ride?" A convertible filled with horny twenty-somethings pulled up beside her.

She kept on moving, even though she could live off their combined sexual energy for a week. "No, you need a swift kick in the ass?"

"Whatever fatty." The car screeched away, the gaggle of dickheads laughing like they'd told the funniest joke ever.

Sigh. Jada had ninety-nine problems, but her curves weren't one.

That very minute every single one of those problems showed up.

Appearing out of the shadows, demon dragons formed into their black slithery snake-like forms around her.

"Alone?" one of them hissed . The sound of its voice creeped her the hell out.

Jada backed away, only to find another one right behind her. She held out her hand, like that was going to keep them from killing her. "No, my coven is, uh, meeting me here. So, you'd better get away from me."

"No." The beast in front of her sniffed the air. "No demons here. Only you."

Well, shit. She was completely defenseless. The only weapons she'd ever had were her teeth and her hypnotic allure. But it was to attract prey, not keep from being prey.

Demons didn't fight with other demons, and humans were food, not threats. She had never needed to defend herself.

"I know kung fu." More like kung food. She raised an fist in the air and took a Karate Kid stance. Her fangs extended, responding to the adrenaline coursing through her. She might not know anything about self-defense, but she could bite their faces off.

Hopefully, they wouldn't taste as bad as they looked. She wasn't into blackened lizard-skin.

The demon dragons snarled and launched into the air coming at her. She ducked and rolled, narrowly missing the outstretched claws.

There was a tree ten yards up the road. Maybe she could scramble up it. What, like demon dragons couldn't climb? She made a mad dash for the tree anyway.

A quick glance over her shoulder showed them closing in on her. Then a great flame burst out over her head and the demon dragons went up in flames one by one, squealing and dissolving into black smears of ash on the ground.

"That was a close one, dear. We almost didn't find you in time."

Whoa. A woman, in a white flowing dress straight out of the Renaissance festival, sat in the tree above her.

Beautiful didn't even begin to describe her. Long flowing dark hair, gorgeous olive skin, rosy cheeks, and a Mother Nature vibe made her absolutely stunning.

For a moment, Jada suspected the woman was a succubus. She was that good looking, that sensual. But a succubus's allure didn't work on one of their own kind.

Had she burned up the demon dragons? Jada didn't see a flame thrower anywhere.

"Uh, thanks? I thought those creepazoids were going to kill me."

The woman climbed down out of the tree, in a floating, graceful sort of way. "I'm rather fond of the term, douchecanoe. My husband says I've got a potty mouth, but secretly he likes it."

No succubus Jada had ever known had a husband. Her kind didn't mate. This lady wasn't a mere human either. Being afraid would probably be the smart thing to do. She wasn't though.

An aura of comforting, nurturing, motherly vibes surrounded the woman in white. A sensation Jada hadn't known for a long time. It hurt.

The emotional ping from her brain sent spikes of pain to her chest and settled deep in her gut. Ouch.

Hell, she was so broken.

The woman walked around Jada, or rather floated as if the wind gently carried her. "I've got something for you."

"You do? That's kind of weird."

"I've been waiting for you to leave that house, those demons, so I could give it to you."

Stalker much?

See, should have been scared.

Jada took several steps back. She was wearing tennies and yoga pants that had never been to yoga, and the woman in white had that voluminous gown on. If she didn't have to go far, she could outrun her. "Thanks again, but, I'm gonna go now."

"Here." The woman held out her hand and let a necklace with a glowing charm, hang from her fingers.

Jada couldn't take her eyes off it. She reached her hand out to touch the shining object, mesmerized by its light.

"Let me put it on you."

Jada nodded, knowing that was the best idea she'd ever heard. She bowed her head and the woman slipped the necklace around her neck, chanting a few words.

The second the charm hit her skin, Jada's world exploded into the light of a thousand suns. It blinded her and knocked her on her butt.

She couldn't breathe, couldn't move, only feel. An energy more powerful than sex and blood zipped through her, changing her from the inside out.

It completely overpowered her until darkness crept in around the edges of her consciousness. Damn it all to hell. She was going to pass out, and then who knew what this woman would do to her.

The woman knelt next to her in the grass. "Don't worry, Jada. You'll be fine. Even better when he finds you."

Another figure loomed behind the woman. Bigger, with an entirely hungry, masculine, alpha energy. He was going to eat her, she just knew it.

Instead he spoke. "It had better be soon. Kur-Jara is on the move."

Jada tried to scream or get away or even move her eyes. She couldn't.

The woman in white touched Jada's brow, strengthening the darkness, taking her consciousness. "I know. But Kaiārahi will come for her. He won't be able to resist. And this time, I added a little protection spell, so the little white witch won't connect to it for a while."

"I love your cunning mind, my heart." The man picked Jada up like she was a little butterfly. "Come on, let's get her to Ninshubur before any of those Galla dragons or the demons she surrounds herself with stumble upon her."

The rest of her kidnappers' conversation faded along with the light and the remainder of her awareness. She could only pray she woke up again tomorrow.

The scent of coffee, frosting, and freshly made baked goods permeated her brain, and Jada sat straight up in her bed.

No, not her bed. Not her room. Not her anything.

Curtains were drawn across the windows, but sunshine leaked in and shined a spotlight a tray on the bedside table. A steaming pot of coffee, three donuts, and a note sat there.

She grabbed a donut, sniffed it, and bit in. Mmm. Sugar. A blessing from the gods. Then she picked up the note. It had only one line.

Always be yourself, unless you can be a dragon, then be a dragon.

Was that supposed to be inspirational?

DUTY CALLS

Ky raced through the water, moving faster than the dolphins, sharks, mermaids, and orcas he loved to play with. He'd stay deep in the ocean all day if he could.

Today, duty called.

His brothers needed his help and he would be there for them. Always.

One of these days he was going to talk the other Wyverns into holding an AllWyr in New Zealand, or on Skype.

Dragons were slow to adopt new technology. They'd only recently talked Match into getting an iPhone. Which was a giant step up from carrier pigeon. How the hell the dude was the alpha among alphas and a total luddite was beyond Ky.

Maybe Ky would stop and flirt with the mermaids on the way back. Those dirty girls were some of his favorite trysts. They didn't have the hang-ups like commitment and marriage the humans were so into.

Mermaids just want have fun.

That's what life was all about. Fun, fucking, and fighting demon dragons. What more could a dragon warrior ask for?

Kiki, the Māori woman who had been his father's last companion, was constantly on his back to settle down, make dragon babies.

Not likely, if he could help it.

Ky slowed as he cornered the Cape of Good Hope to let the great whites chase him and nip at his tail. The little buggers were like puppies running after a car.

He played with them for a moment and then continued on his trek.

After he left them behind, a pull like a current—not on his body, but on his soul -tugged him off course. He needed to go north, up the coast of Africa and Europe to get to Amsterdam, where Cage was waiting for his help. But, the open Atlantic called to him to cross. Everything in him said to get to the States as fast as he could.

He'd felt something like it before, when they'd been hunting for the First Dragon's relic. The yearning inside opened an emptiness like he'd never felt, or successfully ignored.

For a flash of a second, he considered telling Cage he couldn't come to his aid. He didn't need Ky. He had the entire Gold Wyr at his disposal with all their special ops and spy gadgets. They gold dragons would do anything for Cage, they're beloved leader and badass dragon warrior.

Ky had never failed to assist a brother dragon Wyvern, and never would. Whatever was in America, he would investigate after the emergency AllWyr. After all, they still hadn't found that relic. But Cage's call for help came first.

He didn't even make it halfway up the coast of Africa

before half a dozen African mermaids surrounded him, blocking his path.

"Ky Puru, you must come quickly." A frantic voice rang through the water, clear as whale song, and as scared as a Galapagos damsel being hunted to extinction.

Mami Wata weren't generally so flighty, which set off his alarms. He slowed to talk to them and would send some other blues to help with whatever they needed. *"Can't today,* ataahua. *Trouble in dragon paradise. Gotta get to the north right quick."*

Another Mami Wata touched his arm. "Demons. You must fight the demons. We are defenseless against them."

Ky circled to a stop. Demons. In his waters.

Aukati. He'd kill the fuckers.

He had a duty to his brothers, but his purpose on this earth above all others was to defend those who couldn't defend themselves against the plague of demons.

Cage would have to wait. Ky had some demons to kill.

"Show me."

The Mami Wata led him to a series of underwater caves, the entrance marked with their carvings and mirrors. This was their shelter, their home. Chunks of the cave entrance had been torn from rock walls. Debris and carnage from the battle showed him that the mermaids had in fact fought back.

What kind of demons could survive in water? He and merfolk around the oceans had never worried about the *taurekareka* in their realm before.

Ky was a skilled warrior, even with the disadvantage of being on land. He used his power over water and ice to incapacitate the little fucking firebreathers.

If this new demon threat could exist in the water he'd need a whole new strategy to deal with them.

The girls led him through a series of tunnels, and they had to backtrack at more than one cave-in. Their home was destroyed, and there were no signs of the rest of their sisters.

One of the Mami Wata, with a golden tail, and deep black skin, swam toward one of the blocked tunnels. "I can hear them. The demons are taking them away."

She rammed the fallen rocks, beating at them with the strong muscles of her tail. "We have to break through, get to them. Hurry."

"Azynsa, stop. You're hurting yourself." Another Mami Wata grabbed at her sister. A trickle of blood seeped into the water from beneath the golden scales.

"No, help me get to them." She swam forward to slam into the rocks again, but Ky snagged her with his tail.

"Let me, little sister."

She nodded and swished her fins to back away. Ky examined the rocks, found a crack where some had come loose. He blew ice into the crack, widening it, and then put all his power into a crack of his tail.

The cave shook, and debris fell from above them, but so did the boulders blocking their path. Azynsa was the first through the opening, twisting and turning, pushing the stones out of her way. Ky followed scrabbling to move enough of the cave-in to follow.

"I see them. Those beasts have my sisters bound. The bastards. I'll kill them all." Azynsa screeched a Mami Wata lament that erupted across the water.

She burst up into a dry cave hidden underground. Holy cowfish, the girl had some guts.

But, she wouldn't for long if the other shapes in the cave were demon dragons. Ky followed, prepared to ice the shit out of anything black and snake-like. He roared when he hit the air. The Mami Wata crouched, surprised and the demon dragons recoiled.

Didn't expect to see me, did you, fuckers?

Ky slashed the nearest demon dragon into pieces before he even touched down on the ground. The remaining nine or ten divided. Half ran into the tunnels behind them, while five remained to fight. Bad choice.

Water and ice were his allies now. He pulled a stream up from the pool and directed it toward the enemy. He could hardly wait to hear them sizzle.

Ky blew out his ice breath, crystalizing the water, trapping the demon dragons in place, but only for a moment. The interior of the cave was scorching, and more heat poured from the tunnels, turning his efforts to steam.

Dammit, he hated volcanoes, even the ones underwater. Where was a red dragon when you needed one?

"Azza, get your kin into the water and away from here."

The girls were already slipping away as fast as Azynsa could untie them. A few remained, pissed as barracudas, and joined in his efforts to drown their captors. They used their tails to splash jets of water at the bastards. You go, girls.

The demons shrieked and growled, moving their focus from Ky's attack to the remaining Mami Wata.

Dumbasses.

He took out the nearest distracted demon dragon with a swipe of his tail and cut its head clean off. The body became a stain on the rock, the head rolled across the cave floor and plopped into the water.

Sweet as. That got their attention. Two launched into the air at him.

As fast as he could shoot sea and ice, they broke through.

The water hardly phased them, and his icy breath weakened with each go.

He'd be spending a week in the polar ice caps after this bullshit. Right after he sent Match and a legion of reds to—

"*Where are we? What volcano or caldera is this?*" he asked the mermaid.

If she answered he didn't hear. The captured beasts lashed out with razor-like claws and teeth, tearing through his scales and flesh. The heat seeped into his blood and body, weakening him.

He had to end this now.

Ky called to the sea, willing her to give him the last bit of aid he needed to destroy the demon dragons.

Moana, whakarongo ki taku karanga.

The water in the cave gushed in a torrent, sweeping the demons and the Mami Wata into the pool.

Now, they were in his domain.

He swam circles around two flailing demon dragons, slashing them from neck to tail. They evaporated into pools of black goo that quickly dissipated. Only one left.

It used its tail to propel itself up through the water. What the actual fuck?

Demon dragons did not swim, and they definitely couldn't breathe under water. Except this one was doing exactly that.

Not for long.

The bastard might be able to swim, but it wasn't any good and Ky caught up within a second. He encased it in ice and watched as its frozen form, wide-eyed, drifted down past him.

Holy shit. It had gills. No fucking way.

He'd be towing this block of demon ice to Amsterdam. The other Wyverns needed to know about this new threat. As the leaders of the dragons around the world, only they could decide the right course of action together. This AllWyr was going to be jam packed. Cage must understand it was time to take action.

Then he could finally mobilize every blue dragon to hunt any demon dragons in the water to extinction.

Two of the Mami Wata swam up and tugged him toward the surface of the cave again. "Ky Puru. Azynsa, he's taking her."

Shit. There had been five demon dragons left. He'd missed one. Ky put on speed and made it to the cave in time to see the demon dragon dragging Azynsa, shiny new legs and all, into one of the tunnels.

"Let go of me, you ghetto mutha-fucker. I will cut you." She kicked and scratched and spewed insults like a hardened criminal. None of which stopped the demon dragon from yanking her hair-first farther down the tunnel.

The heat hit Ky right where it counted, in the everywhere. The increased temperature zapped his strength instantly. He pushed water into the tunnel, doing his best to follow the demon dragon.

Each wave gave him only a second's respite before it evaporated in the heat. He had to keep going. The demon dragons could not have that mermaid. This one was special. She wasn't full Mami Wata. That language was purely human.

Ky scraped the sides of the rock wall, marking his path. The faster he could grab the girl and get back to the water, the better for both of them.

This heat was killing him, it had to be hell on Azynsa's more fragile body.

"Look, cocksucker, if you're going to kill me then do it. Eat my worthless heart out, because I'm burning to death." Azynsa's voice rang through the tunnel, leading Ky to her. Almost there.

A growl that could not have come from the demon dragon rumbled through the tunnel, shaking rocks of fire from the ceiling. "Your heart is what I'm after, whore. It won't do me any good to let you die. But you'll wish you had."

Who in the hell was that?

Whoever he was roared, sending a wall of fire scorching into the tunnel. If Ky stayed he'd be toast. Literally.

If he left, the girl would have a fate worse than death. He couldn't save her if he was dead too. He'd have to come back for her.

The last of his strength was flagging, and it took all he had to turn and run. He slipped into the water just as the flames burst out into the cave.

The faces of the Mami Wata fell when they saw him without their sister.

He'd failed them. For that he was beyond sorry.

"My brothers and I will rescue Azynsa or die trying."

The nearest girl nodded her head and wrapped her arms around herself. "Azynsa has a powerful will. She gets it from her earth father. Those beasts may have her, but she will make them wish they didn't."

Together, he and the Mami Wata swam back to the open ocean, the water restoring them all. Ky thanked the sea for her help and her strength.

A group of Mami Wata gathered around the entrance of the underwater tunnel. They held each other, searching for comfort after the attack. Two stood guard over Ky's iced demon.

"I will be with my kin within the day, and we can dispatch our

finest to begin a rescue mission. But I'm unfamiliar with the land here. Where do we send our warriors?"

"The humans call it the island of Bioko."

Right in the armpit of Central and West Africa.

"What's the name of the volcano?" Ky knew oceans, lakes, and rivers. Match understood volcanoes. The demon dragons would hole up in the belly of the volcano and needed to be rooted out and destroyed.

"We're in the tunnels below the San Carlos Caldera. This was our home."

"I'll put a call out to my Wyr to help you rebuild. Any blues nearby will be glad to help our sisters of the water."

"Thank you, Ky Puru."

Ky reinforced the ice around the demon dragon. He'd need evidence of their new talent. It was still unbelievable to him. He'd fucking tow it to the AllWyr.

"Wait, one moment." One of the Mami Wata swam up to the encased demon and gave it the finger, shaking her hand and wrinkling her nose. Two others joined her, one wrapping her elbow around her other arm as she flipped off the demon.

"That is a curse Azynsa taught us. She knows many, but that is the most powerful in the land of her father. I hope it brings that beast much pain."

"I'm sure it will." Ky would be doling out worse, making good on these women's curses.

He pushed himself hard to get to Amsterdam, but the battle and the heat of the volcano had left him depleted. Ky continually reformed around the demon dragon, while he fought against the warm Guinea and Azores currents.

He should have ridden the Atlantic South up to the Gulf Stream and to make the journey easy, but it would have taken twice as long. The AllWyr was definitely coming to New Zealand next time.

Cage could fly them all there on his wind and sunshine in no time. If whatever the problem he'd called in the other Wyverns for was resolved by then.

Ky welcomed the cooler waters of the English Channel. In another few minutes, he dove through the canals of Amsterdam toward Cage's home outside of the city.

When he arrived in the marsh around The Lindens he tried to contact his brother Dragon Wyvern.

"Cage, I have arrived, and I've got luggage."

No reply. Strange.

"Jakob, Match, you here yet?"

Match's cranky voice replied. *"For hours. What the hell took you so long?"*

"Meet me at the pond. I've brought a present."

Ky dragged the dripping block of ice from the water then shifted into his human form to examine the demon dragon inside while he waited.

The damn thing was still alive in there. It should have turned to nothing more than a pool of black ink, frozen in the ice. Every other demon dragon he'd ever encased had disintegrated. Why hadn't this one?

Gills, being able to swim, impervious to ice. Maybe they were evolving, or this wasn't a demon dragon at all.

Either way, his greatest weapons in the war with evil were much less effective. If he couldn't drown them in water and ice, he would be no better than a dragon youngling with a toy sword.

"You've been dicking around with demon dragons while Cage is dying?" Match and Jakob walked out past the fountain to the edge of the pond.

Match always did have a way with words. An I'm-an-asshole kind of way.

"This is no regular—" Wait. What? "Dying?"

Jakob grabbed Ky's shoulder. "You'd better come inside."

"What about this thing?" They needed to examine it, figure out where it came from or how it got these new abilities.

They'd had some success interrogating a demon dragon when one of Jakob's lieutenants, Steele, had been fighting for his mate.

The two times Ky knew of that demon dragons with enhanced abilities had attacked were around the time Jakob had mated Ciara and Steele had mated Fleur.

Holy shit.

The attacks were connected to Dragon Warriors' mates. Dragon warriors hadn't been able to find their true mates in almost seven-hundred years. This could be the first real insight they had into the gift of true mates for the greens and how the influx of demon dragon attacks was connected.

The kidnapped Mami Wata must be the mate of a green dragon.

Poor Azynsa.

A mermaid and a green dragon with power of earth, a match made in mud. Literally.

But, first they needed to interrogate the prisoner and find out what they could, so they could mount a rescue.

"The only good demon dragon,"— Match blew an intense burst of dragon fire at the beast-come-ice sculpture, incinerating both instantly, "— is a dead one."

Fucking hell.

"*Huh huh huh ha,*" Cage chuckled in Ky's head. "*Fucking red dragons.*"

Cage's tone was light, but his voice was weak.

Ky glared at Match, then said to Jakob, "Take me to Cage."

Jakob led the way into the manor's imposing front hall with the Italian marble stairway. Gold dragons did love to flaunt their treasure right out in the open.

Cage might have a Victorian fireplace for the reds, a French garden for the greens, and an indoor-outdoor pool for the blues, but they all knew that perfectly temperature-controlled wine cellar was only the façade for the largest treasure hoard among them.

Ky wouldn't trade his place in Kenepuru Sound for this kind of opulence. His vineyards supplied half of Cage's wine cellar, and a cavern hidden in one of the hundreds of inlets in the sound was a better hiding place for treasure than a fancy pants house.

Jakob pushed open the doors to a bedroom suite with a glass domed ceiling and decorated in so much yellowy gold it practically glowed.

Holy First Dragon, one of the biggest, baddest, toughest warriors Ky had ever known looked like shit had eaten him for breakfast and spit him back out.

Cage, pale as a sparkling vampire, leaned against the wall next to a window overlooking the pond. "Damn it, Cage, get back in bed," Match growled.

Cage flipped him off, and embraced Ky in a weak, clap on the back man hug.

"What the fuck, bro?" Ky looked Cage up and down. His brother Wyvern was only two-hundred and a few years old. Barely a half century into his prime and not that much older than Ky or Jakob. So, why did he look at if he was pushing his wisdom years to the brink of six hundred?

"Demon got my soul."

Ky glanced to where Cage's golden soul shard should have

been hanging on a cord around his neck. The sight of only a deep wound sent the bottom of Ky's stomach dropping to the floor and bouncing back up into his throat.

"Bugger me."

No dragon in the history of, well, dragons, had ever lost or had their soul shard stolen. They couldn't be taken, only given. Ky grabbed his own blue shard.

It was every dragon's most prized possession. A small piece of the First Dragon's soul mixed with their own. It gave them the ability to shift from dragon to human.

Jakob no longer wore his shard around his neck. He'd gifted it to Ciara when he'd claimed her. Now, it was his mate's to protect.

When he'd done that, Jakob's powers had increased. Cage's power, his essence, was fading right before Ky's eyes.

Cage leaned hard on Ky, trying to stay upright, show he was still a Wyvern. They had to do everything they could to restore Cage's shard.

Was this related to the attack on the Mami Wata? The demon dragon attacks were getting more daring with each new mate found by a Dragon Warrior.

Ky clasped Cage on the arm. "Tell me what happened. I don't understand how it could have been taken."

Cage finally sat on the bench next to the window. "A succubus, and she didn't have to take it, I gave it to her."

Match huffed, smoke curling out of his nostrils. "What he means is he lost his head over a pretty girl, and in the course of fucking around, lost his god damn soul."

Cage shook his head. "She was more than pretty, dickhead." Then he lowered his voice to speak to Ky only. "We gotta get this bastard laid. He gets grumpier by the day."

"I know some mermaids that would be happy to put out

his fire." One of them who needed rescuing. "Match, you need to head down to the San Carlos Caldera. The Mami Wata are waiting for you."

Match grumbled. "Hell, Wyverns are supposed to have control of themselves. Including their libidos. You're all in your Prime. Act like it."

Match sounded a hell of a lot like grandma Kiki. Except grumpier.

"Speak for yourself. Ever since I mated Ciara my sex drive is way beyond when I hit puberty at a hundred. I'm a walking hard-on around her." Jakob wore the grin of a satisfied man.

Hard on or not, if one of the green dragons had a new mate, one who was in a shitload of danger, they needed to get to rescuing her. "The demon dragons have kidnapped one of the Mami Wata who is half human. She's a dragon's mate, I'm sure of it."

Match let out a string of swear words in his guttural Polish. Then he turned his alpha of alphas voice on. "Jakob and I will go to Africa. If she's a green dragon's mate, we'll find her and get her home. You'll recover Cage's soul shard. You're the only one of us that can track it."

Cage rolled his head back on his shoulders like it was going to fall off. "I need you to go get it back from her, brother."

This was guts for garters. But, Ky would always do everything for a brother Wyvern. "No worries, cuz. Easy as."

FACE TO FACE WITH TEMPTATION

*J*ada paced back and forth in the little room, biting her nails and glancing at the decorative clock hanging over the small desk in the corner.

Tomorrow morning would mark the longest she'd ever made it, one week without blood or sex.

It was also the day she was scheduled for her first busy morning shift serving coffee and donuts at the café below her apartment.

She had never been more terrified in her entire life. Not when the demon dragons had attacked her. Not when she was very little and her mother had died. Not even when Leon – King Leonard, Ruler of the Incubus - had shown up mourning her mother and taken her away to initiate her into the coven.

The woman, or rather, witch, who owned Nine Holes Donuts had mistaken Jada for her newly hired help. Jada wondered if the mysterious man and the woman in white had done that. Until someone else showed up, she would take the job and the apartment that went with it, and keep her mouth shut.

And her teeth to herself.

But the cravings were getting worse by the day.

Chocolate covered, Bavarian cream-filled bismarks helped. So far.

She also hadn't been face to face with temptation. Whatever kind of witch Ninsy was, she was only part human. The other unknown part of her smelled strange. Like a beautiful, but poisonous hemlock flower.

All Jada knew was Ninsy wasn't edible. She was super nice, so it was a relief that Jada didn't want to suck her blood. It made her training and the slow early afternoon shifts she'd started with a hell of a lot easier to handle.

Ninsy had asked Jada to join her for tea every afternoon around one, after the not so busy lunch rush. They had tea and scones together, and then Jada practiced on the cash register, and served the very small trickle of customers under Ninsy's watchful eye.

One customer, or a cute little family in for an afternoon treat, she could resist.

The hot delivery guy was another story. A juicy, sexy, do me in the back of the walk-in cooler while I suck you dry story.

Ack. There she went daydreaming again. Bad succubus. Bad, bad, succubus.

This whole going cold turkey blood and abstinence thing sucked. Not in the fun way.

She had to keep her mind off humans and all their scrumptious arteries and veins and arteries...and veins.

Jada flipped through the recipe cards Ninsy had given her to study and grabbed a blueberry sour cream donut hole, popping it into her mouth. The burst of fruit and sugar exploded in her mouth. These baked goods, combined with anything to distract her brain from the incessant neediness, were the only way she'd made it through the last few days.

If she could work in the back, making the donuts instead of serving them, she'd have a better chance at not eating anyone, or not getting arrested for having sex in public. But Ninsy was protective about the food preparation.

She ate another donut hole. A few leaves of fresh basil in the mix would give these tasty guys a hint of herbal goodness. Not that she wanted to tell Ninsy how to run her business. At least she had a business. A legitimate one.

No other paranormal being Jada had come across wanted to work for a living. Well, she was going to. Didn't matter that she was forced to at this point. There was a sense of relief in knowing that if she put in the time and effort, she could make a life for herself like Ninsy had.

At least she hoped she could.

Jada studied the recipe cards and menu offerings, even though she was on a first name basis with every sugary carby breakfast item Nine Holes offered, until she was too exhausted to think about anything other than going to bed.

Leon hated the day, as all demons did, and used the night to his advantage. He thought the whole emo wanna-be vampire counter-culture was hilarious, and a it was great place to find willing-ish victims. She and the rest of the coven kept whatever hours he did even though she and Portia and the other demi-demons could go into the sunlight just fine thanks to the human part of themselves.

She never had though. Before this week, she'd never seen the sun so many times in her life. She might be half creature of the night, but no one had ever told her how beautiful a sunrise was.

However, having to adjust her schedule and get up at

noon, had felt like gross o'clock. Tomorrow she had to be at work at six in the morning. That used to be her normal bedtime.

Her head bobbed and the crash of trash cans in the alley behind the building jerked her from drifting into sleep. Time for bed.

She had just enough time to get in a good nap before she had to be downstairs to start the coffee pots. All she'd need then was some caffeine and adrenaline to get her through the morning.

Boy, was she wrong.

The next morning was hell on earth.

"Hey, lady. You gonna get us those crullers, or what?"

Yeah, just as soon as she finished shoving frosting up her nose, because gah, the guy at the counter smelled delicious. In a I-vant-to-suck-your-blood way.

"Be right there."

This was the third time she'd refilled their order because every time she got a whiff of eau de sexy golfer boy she force-fed herself half their order to keep from doing something worse.

She'd already gained five pounds this week. What was five more?

The second she turned around with the bag of donuts, minus one, the scent of cinnamon, nutmeg, and O positive hit her in the teeth. "Miss, do you have pumpkin spice creamer?"

Jada bet the woman would taste exactly like pumpkin pie. "Not for a few more months. It's only Spring. Sorry."

She bit the inside of her lip to keep her mouth shut and her fangs hidden.

She handed the order over and the next man in line practically assaulted her and her senses. "You're not out of chocolate raised glazed, are you? That's my lucky donut. I have to have at least two or my handicap will go through the roof."

Early morning golfers were more superstitious and demanding than a thousand-year-old incubus. Sheesh.

"Are you Eric?" The oh, so edible Eric? "Ninsy had me save you a couple. I'll run and grab them."

Run right out the back door and into oncoming traffic. Because a traumatic brain injury might be the only way to get her mind off sucking every single person in the café drier than a day-old donut.

Except it would take her body only a few hours to heal any broken bones, so a crushed skull and some squished brains would only save her from one day of mouthwatering, soul-sucking torture.

Plus, she'd probably lose her job.

She'd been a fool to think she could be around humans without wanting to turn the café into a blood bath or an orgy. Stupid.

Her stomach growled. "Shut-up, you."

Ninsy laughed and shoved a mug of herbal tea into Jada's hands. "Oh hey, Miss cranky-pants. Not a rise and shine gal, huh?"

Ninsy had more burns on her arms this morning. She really should wear gloves or something around the oven and fryers.

"Sorry, I wasn't yelling at you. I'm working on the whole morning person thing."

"Sip on that. It'll get you through." Ninsy tipped her chin toward the cup, but before Jada could say thanks, the timer on the oven went off and the bell at the cash register dinged.

She took a quick scalding sip of the hot beverage and grabbed Eric the Edible's good luck donuts.

A line four deep waited at the counter and she raced to fulfill all the orders. Being ultra busy kept her blood-lust at bay. Or maybe it was that tea.

Either way, she made it through the shift without snacking on anything with a heartbeat. She did owe the till her day's wages, plus tomorrow's and most of next week's for all the donuts she'd eaten.

Worth it.

The only thing left was the plate of strawberry rhubarb Danishes that no one seemed to want.

The café was empty for the moment. Ninsy had said she needed more rhubarb and decided to try the fresh basil in the blueberry donut recipe. She popped over to the market down the street to get her fresh produce.

Jada got busy bussing the tables, refilling the coffee bar condiments, and congratulating herself on controlling her emotions and hunger.

She'd learned one important thing. Leonard had lied. He'd always made her think she'd die if she didn't get regular, almost daily, servings of blood and sex.

The half human part of her was perfectly happy to be on a see-food diet. It was the crybaby emotional demon part of her, that needed a good spanking and to be put to bed.

Ooh. Spanking. Mmm-hmm.

Ack. No. Naughty libido.

She thought the sugar and chocolate overdose was working to suppress that base urge too. Apparently not.

What she needed was a better plan than eating her way into oblivion, and size a hundred and seventeen jeans, to get over her need for blood and sex.

Too bad there was no such thing as Vampires Anonymous. She could sure use a sponsor and a twelve-step program.

Maybe she'd invent the steps for herself. Step one, admit you have a problem.

Got it.

She stood facing the display case filled with the remaining day's offerings. They were as good of witnesses as she could ask for. She raised her right hand. Was that what she was supposed to do? It felt appropriate, so she went with it.

"Hello, my name is Jada and I'm a succubus."

"Hello, Jada."

Jada's mouth and throat went dryer than the day-olds.

Donuts didn't talk, so that meant someone else, someone with a deep sexy I'm-going-to-fuck-you-till-you-scream-my-name voice had heard what she'd said.

The glass of the display case only reflected the bottom half of whoever stood behind her. What a bottom half it was.

Walk away, she told herself. Go straight into the back and turn on every noisy piece of equipment and pretend this guy didn't exist.

He'd go away.

Or not, and then he'd leave a bad review on Yelp, telling people a crazy lady had ignored him.

Damn.

Jada slowly turned while also shrinking down into herself. What in the world was she going to say? She was rehearsing for a play. Oh, hell, could she get any more cliché?

She'd simply offer him a donut and ignore the whole I'm a succubus thing. He was here for a donut anyway. This was a donut shop.

The sooner she got him his food, the sooner he'd be on his way and she could, silently, work on coming up with her other eleven steps.

"Hi. Welcome to Nine Holes, would you like a coffee with your donut today?"

Holy Swiss meringue buttercream. He was even more good looking from the waist up.

Dark skin, tribal tattoos on his arms, and blue eyes that reminded her of the waterfalls coming down into a lagoon at the edge of the ocean. Those eyes went wide, and he stepped back, like she'd shoved him. The bone carving on a cord he wore around his neck glowed with a brilliant blue light.

She'd seen that light before.

The skin over her breastbone tingled and she rubbed at it through her shirt. Oh. The necklace the woman in white had given her moved under her fingers.

Try as she might, she hadn't been able to remove the necklace all week. She took a quick peek down her shirt and the charm that hung at the end of the chain was glowing too.

The customer narrowed his eyes at her and stepped directly into her personal space bubble.

"No, I want the soul shard you took from Cage Gylden."

The closer he got, the more she wanted to rub herself all over him like a cat looking for some snuggles. She glanced outside. Yep. Still light out, so he wasn't an incubus turning his allure on her. Which was the only thing she could compare this feeling running through her whole body to. She'd better get away from him, whatever he was. "Uh, I don't think we have that flavor, but I can check in back."

"Good try. You're not going anywhere."

He grabbed her arm and they both looked at where his skin met hers. A zap of dynamite more fulfilling than any sex energy she'd ever had overwhelmed her. All the bloodlust and need from the morning dissolved and the empty place inside of her didn't feel so hollow anymore.

Scales rippled across his arms and neck, and the head of a dragon tattoo stretched up from under the collar of his shirt, literally moving across his neck.

What was this guy? Not incubus, not demon, not human.

The looked at each other and at the same time said, "What are you?"

A smile that made Jada go weak in the knees spread across the mystery man's face. His eyes twinkled, and he placed one hand on her back and wrapped the other around her waist, pulling her to him. Each place he touched her tingled, intensifying the buzz of the necklace between her breasts.

This must be what the hypnotic allure she used on her victims felt like. Who cared if he was going to eat her? It was going to be awesome.

Adrenaline pumped through her like a syringe pushed it in. Her heart raced, and her lungs worked overtime. But, not from fear. Oh no. This was pure unadulterated, unfiltered, unimaginable lust. Different than the bloodlust she fought against. That had an angry, dark, empty force. The stranger's touch filled her straight up to the top with excitement and butterflies and all the feels.

It all felt so damn good. She wanted him to kiss her. Stupid. Crazy. Why would he do that? One point seven seconds ago he'd been accusing her of theft.

He brushed his lips across her mouth, pushing his bottom one against hers, asking her to open for him. The only men she'd ever kissed were under the spell of the allure. She was still so surprised by his move to kiss her she didn't respond, until he nipped at that lip.

Oh, yeah. She parted her lips and inhaled his flavor. His tongue played with hers, testing and tasting her as she did him. He was sour candy and the sea. She couldn't get enough of him.

She pushed her hands into his hair and returned his fervor as good as he gave. Geez, he was a good kisser.

"Ahem."

His lips were everywhere she wanted them to be and his tongue was doing things she didn't even know she liked.

She was probably a slobbering mess, and he could be running the most popular kissing booth in the universe.

"Ah-ah-ahem."

He broke the kiss way before she was ready. She could go on kissing him for days, and not need food, water, or air.

"Ahhhhhemmmmm. Sorry to interrupt." Someone stood just inside the doorway to the café.

Eek. She hadn't even noticed the bell over the door ring, much less another being in the room. Jada was staring up at her kisser and only caught the person out of the corner of her eye. How long had the voyeur been there?

Her guy flicked his gaze back and forth between her eyes and lips, but then stepped back, turning to be by her side.

Jada blinked a few times trying to get her brain out of the gutter and back into her head.

"I see you're not hurting for sustenance then." Her sister walked up to the counter. She was looking very cool in her dark glasses, black leather jacket and messy bun.

"Portia? What are you doing here?" Leon had sent her sister away, a mini-banishment. Plus, he didn't allow anyone from the coven out into town during the day. Jada had been gone a week without so much as even a sighting of any of her brothers or sisters.

She planned to try to get in touch with Portia someday, but not yet. She wasn't ready.

Portia looked around the café and ran a finger over the top of a table, sauntering closer, as if she didn't care about this conversation in the least. It was a skill Jada coveted.

"Aren't you going to introduce me to your snack?"

The guy placed his hand on the small of her back, all possessive like. "No, she isn't."

The kissy face with Mr. Sexy-pants was great, and there was more going on with him that she'd figure out later. But she didn't belong to anyone anymore, so he could take his possessiveness and put it up his butt.

He was right though. Even if she didn't know his name, and she'd find it out as soon as she found out why Portia was here, she still wouldn't introduce him to another succubus.

Dibs.

He was hers.

Jada shuffled to the side and out of his grasp. He growled, quietly enough that only she heard.

Portia glanced between the two of them and quirked her head to the side. "I've come to take you back."

For the first time, probably ever, she felt a little bit proud of herself. A tiny modicum of the hatred for who and what she was had faded, if only for a few minutes.

Going back to live with Leonard, letting him dictate her life, would only push her further into the darkness.

"Back? To Leon, the coven. I... I don't need them anymore."

That might be a lie right now, but she was doing every-thing she could to make it into truth. This week had been hard. Today especially had tested every resolve she had to give up sex and blood.

"Don't do this, Jada. No one survives without a coven. My month away taught me that. At least I had Geshtianna's coven to take refuge in when I got to the continent. You've got nothing."

"I have everything I need. I'm not going back. I can't live like that anymore." Jada reaffirmed what she'd said with a shake of her head.

Neither of them had to pretend Portia didn't know what Jada meant.

"You still can't change what you are. Why do you continue to make it so hard on yourself?"

Portia's words echoed Leon's. She was the closest thing Jada had to a real sister, but even Portia fell in line with Leon's way of thinking.

"You're the only one I regret leaving, but I'm not going back. I must do this. I want to know what it's like to be human too, not just a succubus."

The stranger grumbled something under his breath that definitely included some swearing.

That was not how she'd intended on telling him she was a demon. Crap.

"I was hoping you'd listen to reason, but since you won't, maybe you'll hear this." Portia looked the guy up and down before she continued. She must have decided he was okay. "The demon dragons are coming for you tonight. Leon won't let any of us do anything about it as long as you're in your rebellious phase."

The guy stepped up. "Tell me now why demon dragons would be after this woman."

STOLEN BY A SUCCUBUS

The power that had coursed through Ky when he'd walked into the café and laid his eyes upon the most gorgeous creature on land or in the seas had almost knocked him to his knees.

He'd followed that pull on his soul across the ocean to the east coast of America trusting his instincts. They told him he'd find Cage's shard here.

It had been stolen… by a succubus. Ky had never met one before and now he was faced with two.

One named Portia, who did nothing for him, and his mystery woman. The woman who lit up his own soul shard.

Jakob had told all the Wyverns how his shard had shined when he met Ciara for the first time. Steele's had done the same.

Could it be possible?

Nah, bro.

Just because the green dragons were finding mates like mad didn't mean there was one out there for him.

He didn't want a mate anyway. It would mess up his life in

all kinds of ways. Not to mention his footloose and fancy-free love life.

There was no denying that he was beyond attracted to this curvy succubus. All he could think about was getting his mouth reconnected with hers and his hands on that plump ass.

He had no idea what force had come over him that had him wrapping this woman up in his arms and kissing the sweet life out of her. She'd tasted of cinnamon sugar and something erotically spicy.

What the hell was wrong with him?

It had to be the succubus allure. Cage had fallen prey to it. Even more reason to be suspicious.

Portia folded her arms and stared him down. "I don't know who or what you are, but I'm not telling you nothing about nothing. This is between me and Jada. So back off unless you want to get eaten by demon dragons too."

Ky let his dragon shimmer to the surface, his blue scales rippled over his skin and his hands transformed into icy blue talons. He blew a puff of frigid air at Portia, and icicles formed in her hair.

"If what you say is true, you're going to want me around to protect Jada."

He liked the way her name felt on his tongue. He was going to like a whole lot of the rest of her on his tongue too. Just as soon as she returned Cage's shard.

Portia smacked at the ice in her hair and Jada stared at him with beautiful wide eyes. They were so dark, almost black, but rimmed with blue. He could get lost in those eyes.

She glanced down at his talons and gulped. "You're a dragon."

Every wise-mind part of him said to be guarded,

mistrustful of this pretty female demon. But, he could be wary and flirt at the same time. He winked at her. "I know."

Portia smacked him in the arm with an icicle. "Then why haven't you been here fighting the demon dragons. Isn't that your fucking job?"

"This is only the second sighting of them in the eastern United States." He wasn't about to tell them he and the other Wyverns had no idea demon dragons were here, much less attacking a lovely, lick-worthy succubus.

"They've been hunting Jada for months. If we'd known you were on this side of the pond, we'd have gotten you to do the dirty work. Those things are disgusting."

If they'd been hunting Jada, then how had she stolen the shard from Cage? It appeared she had an alibi. Which meant she had an accomplice.

It couldn't be Portia. She was as confused as Ky. He would get the answers out of Jada, by torture if he had to.

He could imagine a lot of delicious tortures to get her to talk. Like orgasm denial for one.

He needed to find out what Portia knew and get rid of her as soon as possible. "I'm here now. Why don't you tell me everything that's happened, especially how you know they are going to attack tonight?"

Portia stayed tight-lipped. He turned to Jada and licked his lips.

"I haven't seen any of them since the first night I left and the—" Jada slammed her mouth shut and filled her cheeks up with air without finishing her sentence.

Cute, but suspicious.

"And?" he prompted.

She frowned with one side of her mouth. She was about to lie to him. He scented it rolling off her like the tide.

"I…escaped them."

He'd get the truth behind that lie out of her too. Nipple clamps. Hmm. Surely there was a sex toy shop in this town. He had some interrogation supplies he needed to buy.

Portia drummed her fingers on the tabletop. "They've been here. They haven't stopped hunting you. I saw the evidence of their deaths in the alley behind this place."

How had she noticed that, and Ky hadn't? He hadn't done a very good job of being an investigator. He'd blindly followed his instincts right to Jada.

A succubus couldn't allure from across the ocean, right? Probably not. Something else was interfering with his good judgment.

That something was in his pants. He'd never let lust get in the way of dragon business before. *Get your shit together, bro.*

"Show me this evidence while you tell me how you know the demon dragons are coming tonight."

Portia bit her lip and backed away. "I've already said too much. I'll be lucky if Leon doesn't banish me for real this time. I've got to get back to the house."

Jada grabbed her friend's hand. "Portia, wait. I don't care about the rest of them, but I'd like to know that you're okay."

Portia glanced outside, then between the two of them. She stared for a long moment at Ky, sizing him up. As Jada's protector, or did this woman see him as a threat?

Because he was both. No demon dragon would touch Jada, but she would give him the shard and reveal her accomplice.

Portia raised an eyebrow at Ky but spoke to Jada. "You need to worry about you."

Jada nodded. "I will. I promise."

A tremble worked its way into her voice. It sucker-punched Ky right in the gut.

"How can I get in touch with you? Should we have a secret signal and a secret meeting place?" Jada asked Portia.

Ky recovered by focusing on that potential escape plan. She couldn't get him to give into her succubus ways. Oh no. If he had anything to do with it, there would be no secret meetings.

Jada held some hefty keys to what was going on with the demon dragons and Cage's stolen soul shard. He was responsible for figuring out what those were.

Thinking with his dick wasn't helping. Ky wasn't ready to admit that she had some power over his own shard too.

Nope. Not even a little. His need for this woman controlled his head. Besides that scorching kiss, he'd resisted her allure. He could continue to do so.

Portia smiled and shook her head. "If you're going to live in the real world, you need to start acting like a modern human. Get yourself a cell phone."

Jada wrinkled up her nose. "Blech. Kitchen tech I can get down with. It makes life better. Cell phones are little zombie making machines. Do I have to?"

"Yes, you do." Ky butted in and mentally made a note to get her a phone. He wondered how old she was. She looked around his age, or what humans assumed was his age. Late twenties. But she acted like Match or Nana Kiki, who both refused to get with the times.

He had no idea how a succubus aged. She could be twenty-something or twenty-thousand.

Thinking of her as a grandma helped cool his libido. But not much.

Portia pulled away from Jada, but then hugged her tight. "He took the words right out of my mouth. And get an iPhone so we can FaceTime."

"I know you're speaking English, but I don't understand the words coming out of your mouth."

Portia laughed and moved toward the door. She pointed at Ky. "I've got to go. I'm leaving her in your hands, dragon boy. Keep her safe or I'll drink you dry."

He recognized the threat came from a place of worried love. He wouldn't take offense. Especially since he had no intention of letting Jada out of his sight.

He gave Portia a salute and wrapped an arm around Jada's shoulder. She shoved him off.

The games begin.

The second Portia was out of view, he lifted Jada's chin with his knuckles. "Now, where were we...."

In the last minute, he'd come up with the perfect plan. He'd seduce the information out of her.

Sweet as.

Adorably, she blushed. He didn't think a sexual being like a succubus even knew how to blush. "Ah, yes, we were right about here."

Ky lowered his mouth to hers, taking her mouth, inhaling her breath. The zing of energy he'd felt before hit him twofold this time. He wanted, needed so much more from her than a kiss.

He lifted her by the legs, wrapping them around his waist. She squealed and grabbed his shoulders.

The counter sat a foot behind them and he stepped toward it to lean her against it, fully intending to lay her out and strip her bottoms off.

Her head tipped back, searching for where he was going, baring her neck to him. His muscles tensed at the sight of her creamy skin, unmarred. His for the taking.

As soon as she answered his questions.

He scraped his teeth across the base of her neck, pushing her shirt aside with his chin.

"Oh hell. What are you doing to me? We should not be making out in the middle of the café in broad daylight. But do that again. Please."

He chuckled because that was exactly what was going through his mind too. They should be doing this someplace a little more private, but he was not waiting.

"Tell me where you hid the soul shard and we can take this anywhere you'd like." He nibbled and licked his way from one collarbone to the other, hoping to keep her mind on what he was doing to her body.

"I don't know what a soul shard is."

He pushed a basket of doggie donuts next to the cash register to the side, making room to lay Jada down. "The golden crystal you and your partner took from Cage Gylden."

She leaned back on her elbows which thrust her fantastic rack right into his face. He was going to spend days with his face or his cock between those tits.

"Who is Cage Whosie-whatsie?"

Ky couldn't get to her shirt to lift it up, until he got rid of the apron she had on. No way was he taking the time to cut through the knots. He sliced the fabric tie on either side and pulled it over her head.

"I hope you know how to sew, because I don't, and someone has to fix that, so I don't get fired." She tugged at the hem of his shirt and shoved it up, running her hands along his chest and stomach. "Holy washboard abs. I think I could actually do my laundry on your stomach, it's so rock hard."

She was doing a great job at avoiding his questions and distracting the hell out of him with her touch. "That's not the only thing that's hard, *wahine ataahua*. Give me the shard, and I'll show you."

"You could be calling me an ugly duckling and it would still sound sexy with that accent. Is it Australian?"

"No doll, I'm no wallaby. Think a little lower." Damn, she'd distracted him again. He would get back to the soul shard and where she had it.

"I've been thinking lower, like all the way down in the gutter since you walked in the door. Why is that?"

"You're the succubus. You tell me. While you're at it, tell me where the soul shard is." Yeah, smooth seduction. Real smooth.

"Is it like a crystal on a necklace? Kind of like yours?" She indicated toward his own soul shard dangling over her where she'd lifted his shirt.

"Yes. Do you have it?"

She reached inside of her shirt, and he wished with all his might she was taking off her bra, but he supposed he should hope she was fishing for the shard.

She pulled out a charm tied with a loop on the end of a cord. The shape matched the bone carving his own soul shard was surrounded by a *Manaia* spirit creature that resembled a dragon.

The paua shell at its eye glowed a deep blue, filling the café with light.

This was not Cage's shard.

Ky reached out to touch the necklace but thought better of it. Manaia carried power and until he knew what it was and who'd given it to her, he'd be cautious.

"Where did you get this?" He wrapped his fingers around Jada's hand where she clutched it in her grasp.

His shard was a gift from the White Witch. All dragon

warriors received the gift when they came of age. A piece of their own souls mixed with that of the First Dragon, granting them long life, the ability to shift between human and dragon forms, and the responsibility to defend the world from evil.

How did a succubus end up with one?

"A woman in a white dress gave it to me. Right before she knocked me out with some sort of spell. I think she was a witch."

Not possible. A witch had given her a bone carving identical to his own, that glowed with a light matching the one coming from his own soul shard.

She had to be playing a trick on him, or lying.

But she didn't smell like she was.

Enough. He shifted his hand and touched the shard. It disintegrated beneath his fingers. The bone and shell shimmered and transformed into red, blue, green, gold, and sparkling white dragon scales.

"Whoa. How did you do that? I haven't been able to take it off since the witch put it on me."

"He doesn't need it anymore. He has found you." A small woman with the presence of an Amazon walked in through the back of the shop.

Jada scrambled out of his arms and off the counter putting her clothes to rights, hiding behind him. She'd turned red as coral upon hearing the woman's voice.

"Ninsy, oh hell. We kind of got carried away."

The woman smiled at Jada as if it not matter that he and Jada had been caught with their pants down, but that she approved.

"Hello, my lord Kaiārahi Tarakona Puru." The woman's Māori accent was perfect. But she was no Antipodean. She was also no dragon.

She shouldn't know his full name. Only a rare few did, and they were all dragons, save his own mother and Nana Kiki.

Ky inhaled her scent and found only calm confidence. Her power ebbed and flowed in and around both him and Jada. A pure virginal caress that meant no harm.

"Hello." He tipped his head to the side, studying her. "You can call me Ky."

She laughed and then covered her mouth to stifle it. "You want to be called after food? That doesn't seem like an appropriate nickname, my lord."

Yeah, how many jokes had he heard like that growing up. Kai which was the word for food in Māori, and Ky, the name he preferred to be called. Same -same but different.

"Why do you keep calling me that?" Only during a blue dragon Wyr meeting did anyone call him Kaiārahi, much less my lord.

She bowed her head in deference. "I am but a loyal servant. Your mother sent me."

This was no ordinary witch. Did she walk between two worlds? Maybe she was *Hine-Nui-Te-Po* Māori goddess of the underworld, protector of the dead. "My mother has been gone for more than a hundred years."

"Not that mother." She didn't say 'silly boy', but he heard it in her tone.

Jada poked her head out from behind him. She'd smoothed her hair and had all her clothes back in place. Too bad.

"Ninsy, do you know this man?"

She nodded. "Dragon. I know this dragon."

Ky narrowed his eyes and studied Ninsy. "But I don't know you."

"What you need to know is that we have only a few hours before Kur-Jara's Galla demons are upon us."

"Demon dragons?" Ky looked more closely at the witch. She had burn marks all up and down her arms. Those weren't from any oven. Whoever she was, she'd been defending Jada, protecting her.

"Now that you have found your mate, they will be more desperate to take her and attack in full force."

Umm, excuse me. Found his what now?

BATTLE OF THE DANISH

*N*insy was being super weird. She was kind of an odd duck anyway, but who wasn't? Now she was all mysterious because what's his name... holy crap, she had made out with the dude twice and hadn't even asked his name.

Ky. He'd told Ninsy to call him Ky.

"Did you just say he'd found his mate? You don't mean me, do you?"

Ninsy came over and put her hand on Jada's cheek. A soft energy, like Ninsy's tea, warmed her from the inside.

"You are his mate. Feel it in your soul, dear one. It is a great gift from Inanna and her dragon. You are blessed."

Her blessed? That was a riot. She'd been damned from birth.

"Thanks, but—"

Ky growled behind them and in an instant a huge blue dragon filled the café with its body. The tables and chairs squashed beneath his body, and Jada had to duck to miss his tail.

Okay, so she'd think about being someone's mate later.

"They are here."

Jada slapped her hands over her ears. Not like that would help. "Ack. You can't hear my thoughts now, can you? Get out of my head."

Was this what had happened to all the dragons' mates? They were driven insane by having a dude in their head all the time?

Ninsy conjured up a shield and a sword out of thin air. "It is not even dark yet. How are they out in the daylight?"

"I'm not in your head. I'm merely speaking into your mind. It is the only way I can communicate with you in this form."

Demon dragons appeared out of the tiniest of shadows. In the corner of the café, next to a plant, under a chair. A black creature slithered up any space that wasn't in direct sunlight. There were three or four times as many as had attacked her on the street a week ago.

Oh hellfire. They were all going to die before she figured out if she wanted to be Ky's mate or not.

Definitely not.

Well, maybe.

He was a good kisser.

Which wasn't really important at this particular moment. So why couldn't she stop thinking about it?

The beasts snarled and snapped their jaws. One rolled its head like a crazy demon and spoke in a possessed-by-the-devil voice. "Give us girl. We go."

Ky responded to that by swinging his tail and chopping off the demon dragon's head. Poof. Just like that, it was a stain on the floor.

The other bastards hissed and snarled and basically lost their shit.

"Jada, behind me." Ky snatched her with his tail and shoved her across the counter and into the kitchen.

Demon dragons leapt into the air, their wings flapping, fire spurting from their mouths. There were so many that in an instant they covered Ky's entire body.

He slashed and turned them into blocks of ice, but there were too many. Ninsy's sword cut them down, but as soon as she felled one, another and another took its place.

They both bled from deep gashes the demon dragons gave them and burns covered Ninsy's arms.

All to protect her. She was barely worth saving.

Jada had to do something.

Ky roared and rolled across the floor, squashing a dozen beasts on his back.

She yanked open the display case and chucked raised glazed donuts at the demon dragons' heads. The baked goods in projectile form wouldn't hurt in the least, but maybe it would distract them long enough for Ky or Ninsy to kill them. Besides, raised glazed were not her favorite anyway. Pulling out the tray of snickerdoodle cake donuts with cream cheese glaze was harder.

She took a bite of one and then flung the rest, Frisbee style, at the three demon dragons climbing on Ky's shoulders, tearing at his scales, ripping them off, exposing new chinks in his armor.

Each wound to Ky, Jada felt, not on her body, but on her soul. She didn't even know she had one until now. She wouldn't know, if it wasn't for him.

He was weakening under the onslaught. One of the beasts opened its mouth wide to bite into Ky's flesh. Jada took not so careful aim and tossed a whole tray full of cinnamon rolls at it.

By sheer luck, one went straight down its gullet. It quirked its head to the side, licked its lips with a disgusting slithery tongue and jumped three feet across the room toward her. Its claws clacked on the tiles with each step.

Shit.

Ky was buried under another pile of demon dragons and Ninsy was fighting her own hoard off with a fire extinguisher, her sword lost in the melee.

Jada backed away. The coffee urns were only a few more feet. They'd make a better weapon than baked goods. Slowly, slowly. A sudden move might provoke the thing into attacking.

Ky tossed one of the demon dragons across the café, knocking it into the coffee urns and splatting them against the wall.

There went that plan.

The demon dragon stood up, shook itself, and zeroed in on her.

The only thing left to defend herself was that pile of strawberry-rhubarb cream cheese Danishes. She backed away and tossed two Danishes at the demon dragon.

It snatched both out of the air with its teeth and swallowed them without chewing, and stepped closer, narrowing its eyes at her. Then it stood up straight, its eyes went wide, and it exploded, covering her in dragon demon guts.

Gross. Awesome. But gross.

She wiped the black slime off her face and grabbed for the remaining Danishes. It was probably total coincidence, but when battling evil incarnate, she'd take any chance she had.

Another demon dragon bounded over the counter, narrowly missing being taken out by Ky's tail. It stalked her the same as the last one.

If they were going to kill her, why didn't they just get on with it? This one tried to grab at her arms and then her hair. "You come now. AllFather want."

They weren't trying to kill her. They wanted to kidnap her. Big mistake. Huge.

Jada threw an arm over her face and in her best damsel in distress voice she said, "Oh no, don't take me."

The demon dragon took her bait and lunged for her. She gave him a face full of strawberry rhubarb.

The bastard screeched, clawed at the pink goop on its face. Too late, its face melted right off and before she could say yippee, it disappeared in a pile of goo and ash on the floor.

Well, hell yeah.

Jada bolted for the walk-in cooler where she knew Ninsy had more of the filling stored. She yanked the door open and found eight-quart containers of fresh home-made straw-berry-rhubarb filling.

That seemed like an inordinate amount. They never sold any of those Danishes. Ever.

She grabbed a handful of disposable pastry bags and slopped the filling in with her hands. Three bags took her about sixty seconds and in a battle for life and love, that was too long.

A snip of the end of the bag and her weapons were ready. She hefted one of the full containers under her arm and piled the bags on top, then she ran and slid behind the counter.

This time she aimed more carefully. She had limited ammunition and a lot of demon dragons to destroy. One big squeeze of the first bag landed half the filling down the front of her, but a stream of the red stuff hit the nearest demon dragon. It shrieked, and its arm melted off and fell to the floor.

"Ninsy, catch." Jada tied the end of her second bag and tossed it through the air to her badass boss. Ninsy didn't catch it, because she was in the middle of running a demon dragon through with her re-found sword. The tip of her blade sliced the bag and coated the steel with the fruity filling.

The next demon Ninsy touched with her blade went up in a puff of smoke.

"The filling kills them," Jada shouted.

Ninsy nodded, slid her blade through the red smear on the floor, and redoubled her attack.

Now to help Ky. Jada refilled her own bag and climbed up on the counter. Fire and smoke filled the air around her. Water and ice covered the floor.

She put the tied ends of each bag in the crook of her arm, pointed the spout at the demon dragons, and squeezed. Red goo flew through the air, coating everything in a thin stream of tart jam.

The cry of the demon dragons filled the air like a thousand dying seagulls. Her plan worked to even out the numbers. Finally, she could see Ky's face again.

He was torn to shreds. Bloody and burned. The sight of his injuries hurt her heart.

She'd destroy whoever created these creatures.

Funny, because their creator decided to show up right then.

The entire front wall of the café blew off in a fireball explosion. Through the debris and destruction, an enormous black dragon walked in as if he were strolling down the boardwalk, not the middle of a paranormal war zone.

His eyes burned a deep red, and billows of smoke plumed from his mouth. He spread his wings and took off the roof of the building, including her lone apartment, making room to fit inside.

Holy donut holes. There went the neighborhood.

The demon dragons who hadn't yet succumbed to the power of the strawberry rhubarb gathered around their leader.

A darkness within Jada recognized this specter from hell. The Black Dragon. He was the king of the underworld come to drag them all to his dark domain.

Hell.

Fear wrapped itself around her chest and squeezed. That darkness could easily draw Jada down. She couldn't let it take Ky.

Ninsy was nowhere to be found. Please let her be okay. No way could Jada handle another death because of some price on her head by the ruler of the underworld.

She crawled off the counter and over to Ky. His great chest heaved, and his cuts and lashes seeped blood.

She'd done this to him, and now because of her, they were all going to die at the hands of the Black Dragon.

For the first time in weeks, sugar wasn't the answer to all her problems.

The sun sank in the sky behind the dark form of the King of Hell. Night was falling. More demons would come out to play.

Her kind.

The inkling of a very scary and sad idea formed in her mind. She hated everything about it, because she'd vowed she wouldn't go back.

It wasn't like she'd ever kept a promise to herself before. No use starting now.

She knew what to do. There was no other choice.

Jada leaned back against Ky, drawing strength from his weakness. He'd fought a losing battle to protect her. Now she would do the same.

She raised her hands into the air, palms facing the sky, eyes closed, heart and mind open. "Great Lilith, I seek your blessing. I ask a favor of you if it please you, bring forth the one who lies upon sleepers, the incubus Leonard, with whom I share the pact of blood and lust."

She picked up a broken piece of glass and sliced her hand, letting the blood drip to the ground. "Lilith, please receive this offering. I give it truthfully and willingly."

The ash and smoke from the battle swirled in a man-sized whirlwind. The form of Leonard emerged, half-naked and pissed as hell.

He hated being summoned. Well, tough. She hated needing him to save her. She'd suck it up, buttercup, if it would save Ky too.

"Leon, help me. I'll do anything." What that really meant was I'll come back to the coven and never leave again.

"Your word is your bond, daughter." Leon assessed the situation in an instant and faced the great dragon.

The Black Dragon might be the King of Hell, but his realm did not rule an incubus as old and powerful as Leonard, a king in his own right.

He pointed a long finger at the dragon. "What business have you with my daughter, Kur-Jara. Go back to your corner of Hell. This is mine."

The Black Dragon laughed in the super creepy way serial killers did. "She is yours no more, incubus. She belongs to my world now. You feel it too. Her soul has awakened. I tire of your attempts to keep her from me."

He spread his great wings, blocking the remaining light

from the waning sun. From the shadow a whole new army of demon dragons appeared. They sprang up like scarabs looking for their next meal. Minions with razor sharp teeth to eat their flesh.

There wasn't enough rhubarb goo in the world to defend themselves.

Leon turned his allure on, radiating power, not attracting, but repelling the beasts. They screeched and shrank back from the force of his will. "I won't relinquish her. Her soul is unclaimed, not yours. You'll never have it. Ever."

The pit of her stomach hollowed, being eaten from the inside out. Leon and the Black Dragon were talking about her and her soul. She hadn't even been sure she had one. Leon had kept a lot of shit from her. That would have to wait.

Right now, she needed to put this plan to keep Ky safe into action. She'd let the big boys argue over who owned what part of her all they liked, as long as it kept them distracted.

"Ky, can you move? I need you to shift. I can't move your big ole dragon butt."

He didn't reply. If his chest weren't moving, she'd think he was dead. "Ky, please. Say something."

"*Mine.*"

"Your what?"

A blue shimmer rippled across his scales and he shifted back into his human form. He was covered in blood, and maybe a little jam. If they survived the rest of this day, she'd do everything she could to make up for almost getting him killed. Even if she had to do it from inside Leon's coven.

"You." Ky bowed his head, set one hand on the ground and pushed himself up.

Jada scrambled to support him, putting his arm over her shoulder to keep him upright. "We've gotta go."

"Not yet."

"Yes, yet. You're about a centimeter from dying."

Ky touched her face and smiled, blue eyes dancing like he was having the time of his life. He took a deep breath and shouted, "Incubus, rogue dragon. I claim this woman. I claim her soul. She is mine."

Well, great. Just what she needed. Damned alpha males. As soon as she got him to safety, assuming he didn't fuck it up, she'd be telling him off for thinking he could—

Ky tipped her head to the side and bit down on the exposed part of her shoulder. He broke the skin and a rush like no drug on the planet could provide struck her entire body.

Her mind went haywire and her body went oh-hell-yeah. An energy coursed between the two of them, spinning and swirling from his system to hers and back. Their two became one, linked, together, complete.

Something shimmered across her skin, filing her with light and love and lust.

He released her, licked over the wound and blew an icy cool over it, soothing the skin. The bite had taken less than a second.

She reached up and touched the flesh where he'd bitten her. It was tender, sore, and her fingers grazed across new raised skin.

What the hell had he done to her? She glanced up at him and the lust in his dark blue eyes hit her like the iceberg that hit the Titanic, skidding across her psyche, sinking her. The wounds on his body had healed, the color returned to his skin, and a new power surged around him.

"And I am yours, *aroha*," he whispered.

Fear and worry and despair, and a big burst of how-dare-you churned up from the dark hidden places inside where she kept them. She'd belonged to Leon, the Black Dragon wanted her, and now Ky had taken it upon himself to make her belong to him.

Jada reached out and slapped Ky across the face.

He didn't move but frowned and searched her eyes. "Save that for the bedroom, mate."

The Black Dragon roared and lifted up into the air, flying over their heads, wreaking havoc from above. His demon dragons jumped around, screeching like flying monkeys.

Leon raised his hands, exactly as she'd done to summon him, then fisted them tight and whipped them down, spreading drops of blood from the palms of his hands.

Dozens of her brothers and sisters, including Portia manifested in tornadoes all around them. Leon turned to her and Ky, and mouthed the word, "Run."

Ky shifted back into his dragon form, snatched her up, and took to the air too. He pivoted and dove, while Jada screamed and squealed.

Down below Leon and her siblings ripped the demon dragons to shreds. They fought like a well-trained machine, protecting each other's backs, forcing the enemy to retreat.

She couldn't fight like that. She'd never even seen any of them so much as punch each other in jest.

She was definitely signing up for some self-defense classes, like Kung Fu or Krav Maga, after today.

She kicked her feet, catching one demon dragon in the jaw, before Ky lifted them higher into the sky.

"Hold on."

"To what?" He had his talons wrapped around her shoulders like a harness. Jada grabbed onto them like they were the straps to a parachute pack. It was really going to suck if he dropped her.

The Black Dragon roared again and shot a swath of fire through the sky. It dove for them, its claws outstretched, reaching for her.

Shit, shit, shit.

Ky flipped in the air, and Jada's stomach flipped out. Puking was better than dying.

The Black Dragon missed her leg by a millimeter, slicing her pant leg clean open. He circled around and attacked again.

Ky blew icy water into the other dragon's wings, tilting him off course, giving them a chance to dart in the other direction.

They flew down the beach and out across the water. Ky's grip on her tightened. *"Hold your breath, Jada."*

Ack. She gulped in three big breaths of air, waiting for him to drop into the sea. On her last big inhale Ky dove into the water, tucking her tight against his chest, and sped through the currents, away from the Black Dragon and his minions of hell.

JUST KEEP SWIMMING

Ky slipped beneath the waves and formed a bubble in the water around Jada. She sputtered and took in deep breaths, but then remained silent.

Too silent. It had been evident all over her face she'd known who the black rogue dragon was. The question was how.

Fleeing from a battle pricked at Ky like the spines of a lionfish. He never retreated. A dragon warrior fought until the bitter end.

His people looked to him to lead them, in battle and in life. All responsibilities he gladly accepted as the first son of the Blue Dragon Wyr.

The responsibility for another's soul, that's what he'd taken on when he claimed Jada.

Even in his dragon form, healed of all his wounds from the cool water of the Atlantic soothing him, he could still feel the sting from the slap to his face. He'd claimed her, and she'd fucking slapped him.

She didn't realize the torture that inflicted on his soul. She didn't want him, and he could think of nothing but claiming her again and again, until she accepted him, accepted them.

He never thought he'd have a mate. Told himself he didn't need or want one. There were plenty of women to share his bed.

The feel of her in his arms, when he kissed her, when he'd claimed her, tossed his lonely existence right out and into the dirt to be eaten by the dogs.

He'd never been so completely connected to another being's soul. Could he trust her with his own?

A mate.

Jada was Ky's mate now. He'd claimed her.

She filled his soul with such a sense of rightness, completeness, purpose. He knew, without a single doubt they were meant to be together. Jada not only doubted, she actively rejected the mating.

Too bad. She was his whether she liked it or not.

He may have lost this battle against that black dragon and his legions of demon dragons, but he would win the war for Jada's heart.

He simply needed a plan, and maybe some advice from his Nana Kiki.

Despite his wounds and exhaustion from the battle with the demon dragons the conversation between the incubus and the black dragon had cut him deeper than any other injury.

Jada's soul had awakened. What did that mean?

He knew so little about a succubus, he couldn't even come up with the right questions to ask.

As soon as they got to safety, he would be asking a whole lot of questions anyway. He was tempted to hit the Gulf Stream and straight back to Europe. But, he hadn't yet found Cage's soul shard.

What he really wanted to do was swim all the way back to New Zealand and his home on Waitaria Bay, where he could take his beautiful curvy demon straight to his bed and make her come until she begged to be his mate. Either that or lock her up in his lair with the rest of his treasure.

HE MIGHT HAVE RUN from the fight, but he would not abandon the war against the demon dragons, or their new leader.

He and the dragon warriors had encountered the beast before, when Steele had found his mate. After their last battle with the black dragon, Match and Jakob assigned two of their dragon warriors to the South-Eastern seaboard of the United States.

Since Steele and Fleur had been the focus of the battle with the black dragon before, they could provide shelter and more information. That's where they would go.

Soon the waters would warm as they headed south. This country was too fucking big.

They'd need hundreds of dragons to be able to patrol the whole thing. A few dragons lived on the West Coast, where some of his blues liked to fish in the warm waters, but there were too many people in this part of the world for his Wyr's liking. He'd have to contact Match as soon as possible to get some more reds out this way.

They could send in all the troops they wanted, but until he had an idea of where to send them and what they should do, there wasn't a whole lot of point. He had to find out more about the black dragon.

"How do you know the black dragon?"

She didn't respond.

"You may have information that can help us defeat him."

Still nothing.

"Talk to me, Jada, or when we get to shore, I'm going to spank that luscious ass of yours 'til it's red."

She wriggled around in his talons, kicking and slapping at him so much he nearly dropped her. Maybe he should. Let her cool off.

Yeah, but she'd probably kill him when he got her back to shore.

"Stop fighting, aroha. *I promise not to spank you. Unless you ask me to."*

"Get out of my head, you big lizard."

Big lizard? At least she was talking to him.

"We are going to seek shelter and regroup with another dragon warrior and his mate." Maybe Jada could get some reasons on why to not kill him from Steele's mate, Fleur. That witch was full of sass and more sass.

"Oh, yeah? Maybe she'll show me how to…" She cursed a blue streak.

Her how-to list was filled with such a litany of creative swearing, mostly themed around threats to his balls, that he mentally crossed his legs.

Ky kept his thoughts to himself and when they got close, he chose to fly directly to Steele and Fleur's new home instead of wasting time on land.

He didn't love being in the air like Cage did. But, he couldn't risk running into more demon dragons on the ground. There was also the distinct possibility that Jada would try to run away from him if given the opportunity.

Ky spotted Steele and Fleur's home and circled down to it. Vines climbed the walls, and one corner of the back garden was covered in little white flowers. A green dragon and an earthy flower witch's delight.

At least they had a pond in the back too. The things he'd like to do to Jada in that pond.

He carefully set her on the walkway to the front of the house and shifted into his human form. Instead of bolting like he expected her to do, she stretched her shoulders, rolling her head back and forth.

A blue dragon tattoo, matching his own but smaller peeked out along her collarbone. His mark. The bite had shimmered and swirled forming the symbol on her skin right before his eyes.

There was no mistaking what it meant.

But Jada hadn't yet seen it.

He took her hand, not giving her any more opportunities to get away from him and walked them to the front door.

He expected her to try and yank her hand from his. She surprised him by holding it tight.

Her skin was warm and sent heat up his arm. If he let it, that heat would sink into his whole body. Her sensuality was already trying to work its way toward his cock.

Fucking his luscious mate would have to wait. A long fucking time given the way her mind was freezing him out. Good to know at least her body reacted to his.

A sign on the door with a stylized green dragon painted on it and old-world script read: Here there be dragons.

Ky knocked on the door.

He scented sex in the air, and mentally apologized for interrupting. They waited only a few seconds before they heard voices on the other side of the door.

"Go away." Steele's voice came through the wood.

"It's Kaiārahi Tarakona Puru." He used his alpha voice, not wanting to waste any more time.

"Shit."

The door opened to a cute and curvy woman in a green bathrobe tied slightly askew, with daisies in her sex-mussed hair and an angry dragon warrior wearing nothing but a fig leaf behind her.

"Hi, come on in," she said.

Steele's adorable mate led them into the house with walls covered in living plants. Half-way down the hall she noticed her mate wasn't wearing anything and smacked his ass. "Go put some pants on. We've got company."

Steele laughed and disappeared into another room.

Fleur led them past a tree growing in the middle of the house and into a sunken living room, where Steele rejoined them wearing pajama pants.

She offered an outstretched hand to Jada. "I'm Fleur, and this ill-mannered dragon is Steele."

Jada sucked in a sharp breath and squeezed Ky's fingers tight.

Before, she couldn't wait to get away from him. The scent of a new anxiety wafted from her. She had nothing to be nervous about in this house. These were friends.

He gave her hand a squeeze and then let go, showing her it was okay.

Jada swallowed, pushing a mask over her fear, and took Fleur's hand, but only for a fraction of a second. She threw her thumb over her shoulder indicating him. "Is he as big of a dickhead as this one?"

"Oh my." Fleur laughed. "It's like that. Come on in to the kitchen and have some tea with me for some girl talk. I'll tell you all about the time I made Steele sleep in the bathtub."

Jada hesitated, but followed Fleur. As soon as she was out of earshot, Ky breathed a long sigh. Steele glanced down at Ky's glowing soul shard and clapped him on the back.

"So, that's...your mate."

"Yes. I have been blessed." He made it sound sarcastic, but she truly was a gift. She didn't see it that way.

"Clearly." Steele stepped down into the room and crossed to a built in mini-bar. He poured them both a few fingers of dragon spirit. He dropped ice into Ky's glass and then blew a mist of his healing dragon's breath into both glasses. "Here, you look like you could use this."

Could he ever. Imbued with Steele's healing power, the alcohol coursed through the cells of his body, restoring and rejuvenating. His muscles weren't as sore, and the tiredness slipped away.

His mind felt clearer too. Except in matters of Jada. Only two other dragons in the world had found mates. Steele was one of them.

"When you claimed Fleur, did she resist the mating?"

Steele chuckled and lifted his glass in a salute before taking a swallow. Ky did the same.

"For a while there, I wasn't sure Fleur was going to accept me at all. She was pretty damn sure she was destined to mate one of the wolves here."

"What changed her mind?" It was strange asking advice from a younger dragon, but only Jakob and Steele had been through this mating business.

Steele sat on the edge of the couch. He stared into his glass for a moment. "I'm not sure, and this is going to sound crazy, but I think it was the White Witch."

The mate of the First Dragon. The mother of them all. Ninsy's words rang through his mind. *Not that mother.*

Ky nodded. Steele wasn't crazy, what he'd revealed made sense. "Jada had a necklace. It glowed with the light of my soul shard. She said a witch in a white dress gave it to her. When I touched it, it disappeared."

"Same thing happened to me when I gave Fleur my own shard." Steele touched the place on his chest where his soul shard used to hang. "Do you think the White Witch is, I don't know, matchmaking, from the afterlife?"

"Why now?" It had to have some connection to this insurgence of demon dragons. "We had a run-in tonight with this same black dragon we battled for Fleur."

"You saw it? The bastard that took and tortured Fleur?" Steele scowled and paced the room.

Ky knew this news would cause chaos in Steele and Fleur's lives and he regretted that, but he was going to need all the help he could get to keep Jada safe. "We fought him and his minions. Jada's coven helped us escape certain death. It's why we're here."

Steele crushed the glass in his hand, shattering it to pieces. "I'll kill him."

Something big occurred to Ky. "I don't think it's a demon. It commands them and doesn't care whether they live or die in his plight."

"I don't give a fuck what it is. If it threatens Fleur, we have to destroy it."

Fleur appeared in the doorway and hustled through the room. She took Steele's hand in hers and picked out the remains of the glass. She blew her own healing dragon's breath across his hand.

She shouldn't be able to do that. It was a dragon ability. Another gift from the White Witch?

Had she given any gifts to Jada? She stood in the entryway to the living room, looking bedraggled and so damn tired. She might not want to be his mate, but he would treat her as such and care for her.

"We'll contact the other Wyverns in the morning and make plans. Do you have someplace we can wash up and rest?" Ky wanted to get Jada into bed, and not just because his dick was begging for her attention.

"Of course." Fleur led them to a lush guest room, decorated in a range of colors, with plants, a small water fountain, a fireplace, and big windows, so that a dragon from any Wyr would be comfortable. "There's an ensuite bathroom through there."

He wanted to pick Jada up and carry her to the shower. Fuck it. She could rail at him all she wanted. As long as she was in his arms.

The second Fleur closed the door, he stripped off his shirt, shucked his shoes and pants, and lifted her into his arms.

"Hey, what do you think you're doing? Put me down right this instant." She squirmed, but she was no match for him.

"Don't fight me, Jada. You're knackered, and I can see the salt of the sea coating your skin and hair. You can hate me for it in the morning but let me take care of you."

"No, please. If you stay so close I...I don't think I can control myself. I don't know what I'll do. I don't want to hurt you."

He chuckled and pushed open the bathroom door with his foot. Tucked into one corner he found a huge spa tub. Thank the First Dragon.

"You can't hurt me, *aroha.*"

"You don't understand. With the battle and the week I've had away from the coven, I'm so hungry. It took everything I had in me not to attack Fleur. She's so cute and nice, and I'm afraid some of my allure slipped out."

A rhythmic thumping started on the wall opposite them, and little daisies popped up in the planter box on the high narrow bathroom window.

She gave him a look that said 'see.' "She's got Steele to help alleviate that appetite I might have accidentally increased in her. We have to go raid their kitchen. I need sugar, and a lot of it. If I don't get some soon, I—"

She gulped and turned her face away.

Jada's hunger poured out of her with a scent of smoky need. She didn't want sugar. She wanted blood and sex.

She was a succubus first, his mate second.

He'd been so preoccupied being a whiny asshole about her rejection that he hadn't paid attention to the clues her scent was sending him.

"Let me give you what you really want." He stepped into the bathtub and set her down.

She shook her head and balled up her fists. "No. I can't. You can't."

"I can, and I will."

He pulled her top over her head and lowered his head to the tattoo on her collarbone. He licked it along the place where he'd marked her. She whimpered, and her body trembled.

"Please, Ky."

He didn't think she knew whether she was asking him to stop, or not to. "It's okay. I promise. You can't hurt me. Let me feed you."

She shook her head, her whole body tensed. "I hurt everyone I touch."

Fear mixed with her need adding a pungent smell to her smoky sweet scent.

"I'm not like the humans you've played with. The dragon

part of me won't let you take too much and will heal me. Take what you need. I give it freely."

She bit her lip, hunger in her eyes, and nodded. The tiniest of a smile pulled at her mouth. "I'm trying to give it up, you know. I'm in a twelve-step program."

Trying to give up blood?

She was a succubus. It would be like him forsaking water. Eventually he'd shrivel up and die. But he'd let her have her little joke, if it relieved some of her fear.

Jada leaned into him. "This doesn't mean I'm not still mad at you."

"I know." It was a step closer.

She poked him in the chest. "And we will be talking about the whole claiming and mating thing."

"Yes, we will. Later." He grabbed her finger and sucked it into his mouth.

Her eyes went from dark and stormy to darker and lusty. Her fangs extended, peeking out from under her lips.

He popped her finger out of his mouth and kissed and nibbled his way up her arm. There was no staying away from his mark, and he sucked on her skin there. She wrapped her hands into his hair, scraping her fingers across his scalp.

"Tell me what you need." He whispered and licked the shell of her ear."

"I'm too jittery, too sensitive to, you know, just feed on you. I need to…"

She was reticent to ask for what she needed. She might have never been able to before. If the only sex she'd ever had was with victims, then it was as if she were a virgin.

A really experienced virgin, but with no understanding of the ways of lovemaking.

The thought of being her first true lover wrapped around

Ky's chest and squeezed. He would be her first, her last, her only.

"It's okay, baby. What you need is to come, to take the edge off."

"Oh, I, uh." She looked all around the bathroom, everywhere but at him.

Holy Krakatoa. No way, it couldn't be.

Ky backed her up against the wall and nailed her hands to the tile. She gasped and arched her back into him, still avoiding his eyes.

"Look at me." She stared right as his chest. "Jada."

"What?" Her eyes flittered across his chest, hiding from looking at him. Hiding.

"Sweetheart. Have you ever had an orgasm?"

She turned pink and then red, sputtering out her words. "Of course, I have. I'm a succubus. I mean. I kind of have. I don't know."

"You'd know." He was both angry and excited. How many rat bastards had fucked her and not even thought about her pleasure. They all need their guy cards revoked. They deserved the pain she'd inflicted on them. Now, he had the opportunity to right the hell out of that wrong. He would be her first, her only true lover.

She shook her head. "I'm not usually focused on me. I don't need to get off. It's the sexual energy that I take, not actual pleasure."

"It's time you took both." Ky kissed her, licking across her sharp teeth, and sucking on her tongue. He could go on kissing her mouth forever, but he had a long list of other places on her body that needed kissing.

He worked his way down her throat, keeping her hands over her head. She moaned when he scraped his own teeth across her neck.

Her skin was so creamy and smooth, not a mark on it, unlike his own that was tattooed, scarred, and toughed by the sun and sea. She was delicate and soft in all the right places, a sensual contrast to his hard lines.

He clasped her wrists together in one hand and pulled the cup of her bra down with the other. He'd been daydreaming about seeing his dark skin caressing her snowy white tits, playing with her rosy nipples.

The reality far outmatched the dream. She arched her back into him, pushing her body to meet his. "Ky, I want—"

"Tell me, baby. What do you want?"

"I—I—"

He'd tease her into asking what she wanted. "This?"

He flicked his tongue across her nipple. The little bud hardened, puckering the skin around it. God, she was so responsive. How had no one ever noticed? Just seeing her body react to the simplest of pleasures had his own cock hardening relentlessly.

"Yes, yes."

"Then say it. Tell me what you want."

She whimpered again, in such adorable distress that he almost gave in. Instead, he yanked the other cup down and blew cool air across her nipple.

It hardened into a shiny pink point. "Don't make me kill, you dragon."

"Tell me what you want." He blew on the other breast, sending a shiver across her body. "Say it. Out loud."

She growled at him but then blurted out, "Lick my nipples, suck on them. Right now."

"Good girl."

He pulled one nipple into his mouth, swirling his tongue around and around, exactly like he was going to do to her clit.

Her wrists twisted in his hold as her hands reflexively opened and closed, trying to grasp for something. She slid down the tile a few inches as her knees gave out under her.

It was going to be so much fun seeing her get all hot and bothered. And by fun he meant sexy as hell.

He let her hands escape his grip and they went straight for his head, holding him tight to her breast. She knew what she wanted, or at least her body did.

He reached around and unhooked her bra, then dragged it down her arms as he sank to his knees in front of her.

Her pants were the next to go. They were the soft stretchy kind that hugged her curves. Curves he couldn't wait to see in the flesh. He yanked them down, taking her panties with.

She squeaked and stared down at him, her eyes so wide. He grinned up at her while he tossed her pants over his shoulder.

"Tell me what you want now, *aroha*." He didn't wait for her response. Her musky aroused scent was like a drug. He licked one thigh, then the other, and wrapped his hands around her hips, digging into her lush ass.

He wet his lips and buried his face between her legs, tasting her pussy, eating her juicy lips and clit like he was the one starving.

Starving for her.

DELICIOUSLY SINFUL

*T*he sexual energy flowing off Ky floored Jada. She'd never been with any man who got so aroused from trying to bring her pleasure.

His mouth, his tongue, his hands, were all magic. Everywhere he touched her, her body tingled and tightened. It made her heart beat hard and she couldn't seem to get enough air. It felt so good.

Good wasn't right. Fabulous, wonderful, amazing. None of them described what he did to her. Deliciously sinful was closer.

He made her want more, made her want to feel all the pleasure she'd given over the years.

The power of his lust for her refilled the empty hole in her like fine dining after eating a lifetime of fast food. But this other feeling surrounding him, pouring from him to her, was a force she didn't understand, didn't know what to do with.

The way he touched and tasted her body was a hot meal. The way he wanted to do it and wanted her to like it was the coffee, dessert, wine, and the doggie bag for a midnight snack.

He overwhelmed her, her senses, her body.

His tongue teased, flicking across her clit, but only for a second before he licked his way down to her entrance and pushed inside of her.

Oh, yes. That's what she wanted, needed.

She wanted more than his tongue. Never had she cared a bit about a man's size. She'd seen one, seen them all. His cock was big enough to fill her, and she couldn't wait.

He'd asked her, demanded she tell him what she wanted, but the words felt strange in her mouth. "Ky, take me. Fuck me."

Those were the words men loved to hear.

Right?

Oh god. Now she was all up inside her head. Was she doing this correctly? This wasn't the kind of sex she'd ever had.

He grumbled, the vibrations of his voice tickling her pussy, sending shocks of need straight to her clit.

She had no idea what he'd said, but he didn't move from his position on his knees.

He liked it when she put her hands in his hair and scraped her fingers across his scalp. She did that and tried to pull his head up.

"Ky, I want your cock inside of me."

That got his attention. He looked up, her juices covering his mouth and chin. "Don't worry, I'll fuck you long and hard, but not yet. First I want to hear you moan my name while I suck on your clit."

"Ooh, Ky." Was that what he wanted?

He stood up and lifted her chin, so she could look nowhere but at him. "Don't do what you think I want, Jada. Let go. Feel what I'm doing to you, feel the pleasure for yourself. Not for me."

The succubus part of her was hiding her eyes and pretending they didn't know each other. The human part of her was such a noob. "I am, but I don't know how to do this. I know how to give men every sexual fantasy they have. That's how I get...fed."

He rubbed his fingers across her bottom lip, staring at it. "You don't have to know how. You don't have to do anything but let go."

"What if I can't?" This was too much pressure.

He pressed a soft kiss to her mouth. "Then I'm not doing my job right. Relax."

She bit her lip, tasting herself from where he'd kissed her. "I'm trying."

"Stop trying. Just be."

"But—"

He pressed his finger across her mouth. "Shh. Now lean back and close your eyes."

Couldn't she just bite him and be done? The sooner, the better, so she did as he asked. With her eyes closed the delicious scent of him, of his blood, of his sexual need almost overwhelmed her. There was no way she was going to be able to control herself. She'd just fake an orgasm for him or something. Get this whole experience over with.

She never should have told him she was so hungry in the first place. It was either that or eat their hosts out of house and home. Or eat their hosts.

Ky sank down in front of her, kissing and licking his way across her belly and her thighs. "Lift your leg and set it on my shoulder."

Now she had to balance too? Okay, concentrate. Feel, he

said, just feel. What should she feel? Should she feel happy? Dirty? Excited?

"Stop thinking, Jada."

Busted.

Ky stood up again and Jada wanted to shrink into a ball and bounce away. A succubus was not supposed to be this bad at sex.

"Let's try something else, shall we?" Ky slid the glass door surrounding the tub shut and turned on the shower. Warm water rained down on them at exactly the right temperature.

He turned her to face the water and directed the head to spray across her chest. "No pressure, just a shower. We'll get you washed up, tucked into bed, fed, and you can get some rest."

Wait, was he giving up? That's not what she wanted. Gah. She didn't know what the hell she wanted.

Ky grabbed a bar of soap that had little leaves and herbs in it. It smelled vaguely minty and looked handmade. He lathered his hands and then rubbed the soap across her shoulders and down her arms.

Okay. She could do this.

He spread the soap up and down her arms, massaging the bubbles into her skin. "I liked seeing your arms over your head, your tits shoved out for me to lick and taste."

Good to know.

"I'm sure plenty of your meals have tried to make you submit to them." Ky didn't sound all that pleased about it either.

Uh, yeah. That was a real common fantasy. Although, not as common as wanting her to dominate them.

"But have you ever really felt the freedom in true submission? Giving all your power up to someone who you know wants everything from you." His voice was low and hypnotic. "In exchange, they give you everything you need."

"No." That was not how her life worked.

He brought her arms behind her head, wrapping them around his neck. "I think you'd like it. Not having to be in control."

The bar of soap ran down her ribcage and across her belly, skipping her breasts altogether. His words had a rhythm, like a low purr, soothing her.

"No responsibility for either my pleasure or your own. You don't have to think, you don't have to worry whether you'll come or not, because it's not up to you."

He wasn't even touching her, only the soap sliding along her skin, dipping low, skimming the tops of her thighs. Not hitting her in any of the places she wanted it to.

He whispered in her ear. "You could let go of all those fears, all the compulsion to fulfill another's fantasy. To give so you can take. It would all disappear."

Jada closed her eyes and leaned her head back against his chest. She'd love to feel the way he described. She simply didn't believe it was possible. Not for her, not for her kind.

"I'll tell you what I'll do when you submit to me like that, *aroha*." His fingers circled her breasts, moving closer, but still not touching the places her body screamed for him caress.

"Mmm-hmm." She wanted to hear him tell her. His words, the cadence, the tone, were a balm to her nerves. His touch, on the other hand was building a whole new tension in her body.

Finally, he cupped her breasts, one in each hand and lifted them, massaging with his slick fingers. "I'll spend a good long time teasing these ripe nipples until they're full and tight." A chilly mist of water sprayed right where he'd described, making them do exactly that.

"Yes, like that. Then I'll play with them." He rolled her nipples between his fingers, and his touch shot a zing down her chest and straight between her legs. "Until you're begging me to do the same to your clit."

He pushed her legs open with his, and at first the warm water from the shower swirled across her pussy lips, and into her slit. The frozen mist hit her clit, sending a shiver across her entire body.

Ky's fingers slipped in, circling and caressing her sensitive skin, but adeptly avoiding touching her clit directly.

She whimpered. "Ky, touch me."

He grabbed her thigh and lifted her leg, setting her foot against the wall. She wasn't worried this time about balancing. Ky had her.

"When you're all hot and bothered, I'll spread your legs wide, like this, and look my fill at your beautiful wet cunt. I know how delicious you are now. But I'll make you wait for my tongue."

Another cold blast flashed across her nipples and her hot core. It took her breath away. Ky kept the cold stream on her breast, but at last he touched her where she needed it most.

He spread her pussy lips wide with his thumb and finger, and swiped across her clit, melting his ice and pushing her arousal to a new high.

"Then I'll lick you, just like this, over and over. My tongue is much softer than my fingers. I think you like it a little rough."

She'd had no idea until now if she did or not. Guys liked to be rough, so she gave them what they wanted. Right now, Ky's fingers, sliding over her, pinching and pulling at her, that's what she wanted.

She throbbed, every muscle in her body constricting. She was so close, to something.

"I need, please, please, Ky."

"I know you do. I'm not ready to give it yet."

A groan escaped from the depths of her lungs. She wanted to be mad at him for holding back what she wanted, but at the same time, it spiraled that need deeper.

"Because remember, you've given me the control. I get to decide when and how you get what your body is craving."

Yes. She was so damn tired of being in charge or not, giving as much energy as she took. It wasn't like that with Ky. The energy between them now was easy, so much so that she'd hardly noticed how it was filling her up, giving her a new vitality no victim ever had.

Ky's fingers moved faster, and she thrust her hips forward, reaching for him. Her pussy fluttered. She could feel the tension growing more and more taut.

"Oh hell. Ky. Ky. Ky."

"That's it, baby. Let go, let it take you."

Her body shook and shivered, the fangs she'd forgotten about extended from her mouth, piercing her lip. She could taste Ky already, his hot, sweet desire for her whirled around them both.

"Give in, Jada. Give me your orgasm."

Her body bowed with the pressure until she exploded, her muscles spasmed, gripping her so tightly she couldn't breathe, couldn't see, couldn't move except for the jerking of her hips.

A wave of pure blissful energy satisfied the aching void inside of her. Eroding away at the emptiness.

Her body relaxed, and she opened her eyes to a brilliant blue light filling the small bathroom.

Holy shinola. He was right. She would have known. If that's what having an orgasm was, she definitely would have fucking known if she'd had one before.

Ky helped her lower her leg and twisted her to rest in his arms. He rubbed her back and guided the water to wrap around her like a warm blanket.

"That was damn gorgeous, and I want to see it all over again. But this time, you take what you need from me too."

She opened her eyes. His radiant amulet hung right in front of her face. The glow was cool and bright and gave her that same feeling of satisfaction that his touch had.

He wanted her to feed on him.

She wasn't sure she even needed to anymore.

Water rushed up between her legs again, a steady stream of pleasure. Oh. Ooh.

He swirled the stream around, up and down, rhythmically, the jet pulsing, hitting her in just the right place.

She wrapped her arms around Ky's neck and tucked her head against his chest. He held her tight and pushed her body beyond what she knew it could do.

He just kept building her up and up, the water flowing over her faster and harder with each breath.

"Come for me again, come, Jada."

She turned her head and sank her teeth into the sensitive skin of his neck. She had to trust him now, trust that he wouldn't let her take too much, wouldn't let her hurt him.

The instant his blood touched her lips her body exploded, sending her mind flying, racing, shattering into a million tiny bits of pleasure.

The flavor of him in her mouth, the touch of his body

against her, the scent of his arousal in her nose, and the sound of his voice as he growled her name, all pushed her higher.

"Yes, Jada. Fuck, yes, baby."

Her body didn't stop, sucking up not only his blood, and the sexual energy, but all the pleasure she'd been denied for hundreds of years.

She shook, again and again, even as he slowly weakened the stream of a water flowing across her pussy.

She pulled her mouth from Ky's neck and licked over the wound she'd given him. A peace she hadn't known before curled around her, giving her respite from the intensity of her orgasms.

She could drift in that serenity forever.

Ky turned the shower off and snagged a warm towel from the wall. Steam caressed her skin. He rubbed her dry and moved to get out of the tub, but she clung to him, not wanting what had happened to end.

"Shh, shh, shh. I'm not going anywhere without you. Let's get to bed, where I can hold you in my arms."

He picked her up and carried her to the bed. She was no small thing, but he lifted her like she was a bit of fluff.

This had to be the first and last time she let him do anything like that. She might have given him the control in the shower, but that was over. In the morning, they'd need to talk about the whole claiming thing.

But, later. She snuggled into his arms and was asleep almost instantly.

She woke hours later to an empty bed. She didn't even remember falling asleep. She reached her arm out to where Ky should have been.

Dumb dragon.

More like stupid succubus.

Men only wanted one thing. Except, had Ky even… no, he hadn't. She was the one who'd had her mind blown, her body mastered.

The ever-present hunger that ate away at her insides and her soul wasn't there this morning. Dragon's blood?

It couldn't be only that, or any incubus or succubus who knew would give up human blood forever. Come to think of it, when she'd bitten Ky, it wasn't out of hunger, only the passion of the moment.

Her hunger had subsided before that.

It wasn't the orgasm either. Although, what the fudge-balls? Why hadn't anyone ever clued her into that part of sex? Three hundred-ish years of orgies and moregies, and not once.

Not once!

But, every incubus she knew went on and on about orgasms and how hard and long they'd come. It was completely annoying. Maybe it didn't work the same for female demons.

Now she wished she had a phone to call Portia and have some girl talk. Oh, god. If Portia was even still alive.

Were any of her coven still alive?

Jada scrambled out of bed and went in search of her clothes. She'd had them last in the bathroom.

A quick glance told her they weren't there. Only a couple of towels, some still wrapped toothbrushes, and travel size tubes of toothpaste.

She grabbed one of each, loaded it up, and shoved the brush in her mouth. That's when she caught her reflection in the mirror.

The waves in her hair were springier, and it shined. Her skin wasn't as pale as usual, and her eyes were brighter. None of that caught her attention like the brand new, bright blue dragon tattoo stretching across her collarbone.

It was right where Ky had bitten her, marked her, claimed her.

Her soul is unclaimed.

That's what Leon had said.

The Black Dragon had wanted her. Was that why Ky claimed her? To save her from becoming the consort of the King of Hell?

There were too many questions down that path, and she wouldn't get any of them answered by standing around naked with a toothbrush hanging out of her mouth.

She brushed her teeth, found a hairbrush and ran it through her locks, and splashed some water on her face. It would have to do.

No clothes. Okay, a bedsheet toga it was then. She'd just ripped the top sheet off and wrapped it around her when Ky came back with coffee and donuts. Bless whoever raised that boy right.

"Hey. I thought you might be hungry."

Strangely, she wasn't. Not for donuts, not for blood. Her mouth watered only for a taste of Ky.

Oh, no you don't brain. Don't be going all mushy now. One claiming and an orgasm or two does not a happy ever after make.

Coffee. She needed coffee and clothes, not a sexy dragon to take her to bed and have his way with her. Again. And again.

Ack. Stop it, brain.

"Thanks." She took one of the cups of coffee from him, mostly so she had something to do with her hands and somewhere to look besides his yummy muscles under that tight t-shirt he wore. "Do you know where my clothes got off to?"

"Fleur says they weren't salvageable. She mentioned something about something toxic on them."

That toga was looking more like a reality. "Crap. Why are yours all perfectly fine?"

"Whatever I've got on when I change into my dragon form is exactly the same when I return to my human state. It's part of the gift of the shift given to all dragon warriors by the White Witch."

She had to be the same woman in white who'd given Jada the necklace. Why was a whole other question.

"Fleur said she'd let you raid her closet as soon as you were up. I came to get you because the other dragon warriors are on their way."

Great. More controlling alpha males. Exactly what she needed in her life.

THANKS FOR THE ORGASMS

$\mathcal{K}$y had never had an awkward morning after like this before. Jada didn't seem to care one whit about last night.

No good morning kiss, it's not you it's me speech, not even a get the hell out. Not like he expected tears or words of devotion or anything, but maybe some thanks for the orgasms.

Jada tucked the sheet tighter around her and headed for the door. "I'd like to find out what happened to the rest of my coven after we escaped."

"I'll find you a phone, so you can get in touch with Portia."

"I don't have a number for her or know if she's even alive."

Of course, she was worried about her family. They'd come to her rescue even after she'd tried to leave them. The demon she'd summoned knew exactly who or what the black dragon was.

Jada knew too. It knew things about her, wanted her and her soul.

With anyone else he'd be suspicious. If his head was on

straight he would have already questioned her to find out everything about her connection to the beast.

Maybe he'd been played by a masterful succubus to get what she needed. Some sex and blood, and now she could go running back to her coven, or the black dragon.

"How long till the dragons get here? I'm a disaster area." She tried patting down her hair.

He liked seeing it all messed up. "Just a few minutes. Fleur is waiting for you."

The way she came apart only after she let go, the way she quit trying to be in control of all the pleasure, he didn't think she faked that.

The alternative poked at his psyche like a spear gun. She didn't want to be mated to him and was ignoring everything that had happened between them.

That hurt, but not enough to give up.

She was the one person in the world made especially for him, brave and beautiful and so smart.

Ky didn't deserve such an incredible gift. He'd do his damnedest to be what she deserved.

She was his mate no matter what. He needed to let her come to him, make the decision that she wanted to be with him.

They were good together, better together, and he had to show her. He wasn't sure how he was going to do that though.

Fleur met them halfway down the hall and dragged Jada away. "I think I have exactly the right thing for you."

Jada shot him a look over her shoulder that said she wasn't so sure about letting Fleur play dress-up doll with her.

Ky joined Steele in the living room and Jakob arrived a few minutes later.

"Got here as soon as I could. Damn that flight across the

Atlantic sucks. Thank the First Dragon for the wind, or I'd be sunk in the middle of the ocean."

"Nah, bro, my blues would have pushed your tired ass here." Ky clapped Jakob on the shoulder, glad to see him. He'd have some insight into this mating business.

The first time the AllWyr council had met Ciara, Ky'd have sworn she hated Jakob's guts.

Now they were disgustingly kissy face every time he saw them together.

Jakob had won Ciara over after he'd kidnapped her, held her captive, and married her without her consent. Which all sounded pretty damn bad.

All Ky had done was suspect Jada of stealing Cage's soul shard.

She'd been fierce in the battle yesterday, and damn inventive with the lack of weapons at her disposal.

He'd be dead right now if she hadn't smoked so many of the demon dragons. When Jakob and Dax arrived, Ky would have her take charge of developing the plan to defeat the black demon dragon. She knew the most about that thing.

But she was a succubus. What if she had stolen Cage's shard? She had knowledge of things the rest of them didn't about the demon dragons and the black beast. She could be working with them.

Letting her be in charge would put them all at risk. It would also show her that he had faith in her. He hoped she'd see it that way, trust him.

Jada came into the room wearing a deep blue shirtdress that emphasized the ring of blue around her dark irises. The sight of her in his color took his breath away, locked it up, and swallowed the key.

"Hi."

Yep. That's all he had. No words for how stunning she looked.

She quirked one side of her mouth into a smile and looked at him sideways. "Hi."

His mouth wanted the next words out to be about going back to their room and seeing how good she looked with the blue dress unbuttoned and pushed off her shoulders, so he could see her mark and her tits.

His brain kicked into gear before that could come out. "You look fucking amazing in that color."

He sounded like a dumbstruck teenager.

Jada looked down at the clothes and shrugged. "Oh. Thanks. I'm used to wearing black all the time. This feels like I'm wearing a neon sign that says look at me."

"I'm looking." Ky couldn't take his eyes off her.

"Uh-oh. I should have warned you not to give her a dress that color. He's going to be distracted all day." A gorgeous blond with more curves than Marilyn Monroe crossed the room and took Jada in a big hug. "I'm Ciara, Jakob is my mate. I'm so frickin' excited you're here with Ky. Now I have someone else to be a bridesmaid at the giant wedding I'm throwing…in my mother's face."

Ky shot a look at Jakob, who grinned like his mate had just said the most brilliant thing on the planet.

Love struck fools, the both of them.

"Oh, I…uh, we…" Jada's stumbling over the words to deny that they were together made Ky even more sure he had to go ahead with his plans to put her in charge.

Dax, the red assigned to this area along with Steele walked in and rubbed his hands together. "Let's get this party started. I'm ready to burn up some demon dragons."

"What about Match and Cage?" Steele asked.

Jakob shot Ky a quick glance. They'd all decided not to let Cage's precarious condition out to the dragon warriors. "Cage is indisposed and I'm still waiting on an update from Match. He's in Africa working on this problem from the underground side of things."

If anyone could rescue the Mami Wata girl from the hellish environment of a volcano, it was Match. He thrived in that heat.

Ky offered Jada a seat. "We'll work with what we've got here now and call in reinforcements when we've got a plan."

Fleur came in with a tray of coffee and herbal teas. The pendant around her neck glowed a little brighter this morning.

Ky glanced from Fleur to Ciara and back again. They both wore the crystal pendants. Their mates did not. Both Jakob and Steele had given their soul shards to their mates.

That couldn't simply be a green dragon thing. The shard contained a piece of their souls. No smart dragon was ever without that most prized possession.

Ky knew all the way to his core that they'd given up their shards because they'd given their mates their souls, both figuratively and literally.

He'd give his to Jada a hundred times over. If she'd take it.

They weren't ready. She wouldn't want it, wouldn't understand what giving it to her would mean.

Time to put that plan to win her over into action. Jada sat on the edge of a chair and Ky stood behind her, putting a hand on her shoulder. "I suggest we let Jada lead. She's good in battle and knows more about our enemy, his weaknesses, unlike any of the rest of us."

The room erupted with cries about allowing a demon to

even be there, much less take any charge. Only Steele and Fleur knew that Jada was Ky's soul mate.

Ky stepped to the center of the living room and raised his hands, sending out a wave of cool mist to hit them all in the faces and got their attention.

His powers came easier to him now, ever since he'd walked into that donut shop and laid eyes on Jada. His tactic got everyone to shut up almost instantly.

"I would rather have addressed this later with the AllWyr council, but you lot will have to do." Ky didn't know how Jada was going to react to his announcement.

"Before you all flip your shit, you need to know Jada is a fierce warrior who is being hunted by the demon dragons. The black beast wants her himself. That can never happen, because Jada is my true mate." The shard on his chest glowed with a blue light that filled the room as if to emphasize his point.

Ciara gave Jakob a see-I-told-you-so look and Dax threw his hands up in the air and rolled his eyes. The only reaction Ky cared about was Jada's

Her eyes went wide, and she shook her head at him. She was going to deny it right here in front of everyone. That was going to hurt like a son of mother ducker.

"I'm not a warrior," she said.

The beats his heart needed skipped along in his chest, putting the rhythm up a notch. She hadn't said she accepted him, but she didn't refute his claim either. He could kiss the hell out of her right then.

He settled for staring at her lips and imagining all the fun things he was going to do with them later. "You are. You took out dozens of demon dragons yesterday."

She pulled away from him and wrapped her arms around herself. "By accident."

Was she kidding? "By quick thinking in a crisis situation. We might not have escaped if not for you and your family."

Dax butted in. "Have you always fought those bastards? What can you tell us about the big black demon dragon?"

Jada shook her head again. "I've never fought them before, but Leonard, my father, said they've been after me for months. I don't know what to tell you."

Ky put a hand over hers, trying to let her feel his support. "When we battled the horde of demon dragons and the black dragon appeared, you knew who he was, didn't you?"

She frowned at him. "You don't?"

Steele stood and began pacing. "We encountered him once before, but he is a new enemy to us."

Jada's frown deepened, and she looked around the room at each of the warriors. "But you, the dragon warriors, have been battling the demon dragons for centuries."

Jakob nodded at her. "Yes, but not the big black demon who takes our form and has the same powers as some dragon warriors. We've never encountered any demon dragon like this. It must be behind this new surge of attacks."

"He isn't a demon at all. He rules a section of hell, along with the Black Witch, Ereshkigal."

"The crone," Fleur whispered. She shivered and went straight into Steele's arms. A vine of thorns popped up around their feet.

"We know none of this. Why are your kind hiding the black dragon and the crone from us?" Steele's voice turned hard and accusing.

Scales rippled across Ky's skin, and his dragon shimmered.

Nobody threatened his mate. Not even another dragon warrior. "Watch yourself, green."

Jada got up from her chair and stood between the two of them. She had one hand over her collarbone, right where his mark lay.

"I'm not hiding anything. We don't have that much interaction with him or his kind, but Leon talks about them and your war with them. This is all common knowledge in the demon world as far as I know. Ask anyone in my coven." She rubbed her mark. "I don't understand how you could have been mortal enemies with the demon dragons for so many centuries and not have any information about them."

Dax pounded his fist on the table. "All we need to know is that they wreak havoc on the world, eating people and causing plagues. They are evil and need to be destroyed. Every last one of them."

Reds and their one-track mind when it came to killing demon dragons. That may have worked in the past, but things were changing. This new enemy wouldn't be defeated by brute force alone.

They needed to use their brains.

Jada sat back down. "They know a truckload more than that about you."

Or smarter heads, like Jada's.

Jakob whispered something to Ciara. She nodded and crossed the room, sitting next to Jada.

Jada tensed up making Ky wary too, even though he knew Ciara wasn't there to harm her in anyway.

She took Jada's hand in hers and just like that the tension in the room dropped a couple of notches. "What about this black dragon thing. If he isn't a demon, what is he? Are there more than one of his kind? What do you know about him?"

Jada tilted her head and studied Ciara for a moment. Ky could see a question on her face, but she didn't ask.

"His name is Kur-Jara, and he is the king of hell."

She said it calm as could be. Ky's gut told him this was a big deal, that they should all be up in arms over this information. He understood it mattered, but he was able to keep a clear head about it.

Jakob stared down at his mate, and they could all scent the powerful sense of pride he carried for Ciara. Her powers, those of a white witch, worked a treat to keep everyone focused. Even Dax's hot temper had cooled.

Ciara put her other hand over Jada's and gave her an encouraging smile. "Yikes, what does that mean?"

Jada grinned, shook her head a little. She was as calm as the rest of them, but Ky would bet half his treasure she understood what Ciara's gift was doing to her and the rest of them.

"Exactly what I said. Kur-Jara rules over the underworld. Anything in that realm is subject to his command."

Ciara glanced between Jada and Ky, the tiniest flash of worry crossing over her face. It was gone in an instant, but it had been there, allowing Ky to feel his own worry. "Does that include you?"

"I'm only half demon and I'm not from his realm. I was born to a human."

Half demon, half human. Was that all? Ky felt like there was something more to her. He couldn't put his finger on it. His shard buzzed against his chest. He placed one hand over it and the other softly on the back of her neck, showing his confidence in her through his touch.

She leaned into him and took a breath that he could tell re-centered her.

Ciara continued asking questions they all wanted to know

the answers to. "The demon dragons that he rules, where do they come from?"

"They are his offspring. The product of his union with Annunaki demons. We don't associate with either of them." Jada wrinkled her nose.

Ciara frowned. "They're his evil spawn kids? That's horrible in so many ways."

Fleur joined the other two mates. She worried a green leaf between her fingers, but that was the only sign of any anxiety. "He captured me when Steele and I first met. But, I still don't know what he is, who he is. Why is he after us?"

Jada looked to Ky, asking him with her eyes to end the questioning. She'd had enough, and Ciara's gift was wearing thin.

He squeezed the back of her neck and gave her a small nod. She could do this.

She lifted her chin and nodded back. "I don't know. Leon didn't tell me why, only that he and my coven had been protecting me from them."

"We'll protect you now." Ky wouldn't let anything happen to her. He'd hide her away with the rest of his treasure if he had to.

Even with all this new information from Jada, they didn't have enough. He tapped his fingers on the arm of the chair. "What are we missing? There is a connection between the appearance of Kur-Jara and the mates. It's been seven hundred years and then bam, three mates in as many months."

Jada turned to Ky and raised an eyebrow at him. "Dragons haven't had mates in all that time? Come on, you all are as horny as any incubus. There are dragon sons all over the world. You've had mates."

Ciara and Fleur widened their eyes at Jakob and Steele.

This was like a bad version of the how many ex-girlfriends talk.

Jakob found his dragon balls first. "Companions, yes. But never a true mate. Ciara was the first in several generations."

"You bet your ass I was. Any dragon sons I need to know about, mister?"

Jakob laughed. "Thank goodness for the Earl of Condom."

"What happened seven hundred years ago to keep you all, and presumably your fathers from finding true mates?" Jada asked.

Even Ciara's gifts couldn't keep the dragon warriors in the room from falling somber.

Ky cleared his throat. "The death of the First Dragon."

WITCHES AND WISHES

*J*ada's insides were alternating between tingling and balling up like a fist in her stomach. She didn't want to like Ky so damn much. He'd claimed her and marked her without so much as a dinner and drink.

That had pissed her off. She was tired of feeling like someone else owned her. For once in her life she'd like to make her own damn decisions.

He'd taken the choice away from her again when they escaped into the ocean and come to his friend's house.

That was three strikes against him. One for the claiming, one for the marking, and one for the forcing her to abandon her coven to fight the horde.

Then he went and got all dominant in the shower. Not in a way that felt like she'd given up her power again. No, he'd given her the chance to not be in charge of either his pleasure, which was weird and wonderful, or her own.

He'd said it would feel freeing.

He had no idea.

She'd give him one point, but he'd made her come twice at least. To be fair, she had to give him a point for each.

That still put him in the negative this morning. She'd successfully kept him there through their awkward morning-after, all the way until he'd announced to the whole group she was his mate.

Should have been a strike against him. Instead her insides had gone all mushy and warm.

Damn it.

One point for him again. Made them even.

Fine. She could handle that.

What blew her mind was the way he continued to let her do the talking the rest of the meeting with the other dragon warriors and their mates, all powerful beings in their own right. In fact, he'd encouraged her to take charge.

It seemed like something so trivial, but nobody in her world treated her that way, let her lead, make important decisions that affected the group. Leon and the coven treated her with soft fluffy kid gloves.

Jada hadn't realized that until now. She couldn't fight because she hadn't ever needed to. Same went for making her own decisions.

She hadn't even really made the decision to leave the coven by herself. Leon had pushed her into it.

Today, in the past few hours. The only butting in that Ky had done was to ask questions and say he would protect her. Even when she'd mentally tried to ask him to speak up he'd simply lent her some of his strength.

One thousand bonus points. The bastard. She couldn't be mad at him.

"The First Dragon had a mate, didn't he?" Jada had an idea who that mate was. "A woman in white, perhaps?"

Ky nodded. "Yes, the White Witch. She left us too when the First Dragon died."

A white witch, one who commanded all the elements. There were legends of an ancient battle between the white witch and her sister. "I think I met her, and her mate was with her. He definitely wasn't dead."

Every face in the room stared at her, a few with slack jaws.

Ciara broke the silence first. "I believe I've interacted with her too. She's the one who helped me understand my gifts."

If Jada was right, Ciara didn't really understand the depth of her powers. There were witches all over the world, some who liked to summon demons like incubus, but most were healers, herbalists, and normal every day women. None commanded more than one element. "You're a white witch like she is."

Ciara grinned. "You've figured me out then."

"What you do feels almost like an allure. I thought at first you were part succubus, but there's no draw, no need in what you were doing."

"I can do that, but I save it for Jakob." She winked.

A ping stung the back of Jada's throat seeing the want and need the two exchanged between each other in only a glance. It took her a second to continue. "Your gift in calming every-one's emotions had a similar feel to the spell the White Witch worked on me."

"I'm still learning about my own powers, but the strongest part has something to do with the emotion part of it. Positive ones work better for me, like trust and love." Ciara glanced at Jakob with those emotions and more in her eyes.

Jada wanted to test her theory that Ciara had control over all the elements. "What other powers do you have?"

"I'm a fan of the earth elements, along with Fleur." The

same daisies that had surrounded the house and appeared in Fleur's hair pushed out of the planter nearest Jakob and stretched their little white heads to him until they wrapped around his arms.

He grinned and those green eyes of his twinkled for Ciara.

Fleur giggled like she and Ciara shared an inside joke. "Hey, I showed you that one. It's supposed to be for the bedroom only."

Jakob plucked the flowers and pushed one into Ciara's hair, above her ear.

"Your gift with the wind helped us get here a lot easier," Jakob said.

Ky glanced over at Ciara with surprise. "The gold dragons didn't help you at all?"

The last time Ky had been around Ciara she'd created a fierce tempest that could blow them all around like feathers. But she didn't have a lot of control over her powers with the wind or rain then.

Jakob shook his head. "Nope, it was all Ciara."

She waved her hand, dismissing Jakob's boast. "Well, not all me. I'm sure."

Jada had an answer to half her question. "What about the other two? Fire and water?"

Ciara closed her eyes and everyone's coffee and tea froze solid.

Dax turned his cup upside down and shook it. Nothing came out. "Hey, I was going to drink that."

He turned the cup upright and blew a tight stream of fire at the ice, warming it back up and took a sip.

Before anyone else could say anything, their cups all began to steam.

Ciara blew out a breath and yawned. "Only little parlor

tricks, but they take a lot out of me. I haven't properly learned to focus the elements together , except for that one time."

Ciara paled for a moment and swallowed like she had something bitter in her mouth. Jakob took her hand and squeezed.

They weren't telling her something. Almost like it was a private moment between the two of them. A mate thing. A tiny – okay a big pang of hunger hit Jada. It wasn't for food, or blood. This was something new. She was hungry for that kind of love and connection.

She snuck a glance at Ky, the one being in the universe that maybe she could find that in. He was staring right back at her. The blue of his eyes swirled with the same light in his shard.

The hollow part of her, where she wasn't totally sure her soul lived, claimed the look in his eyes reflected the same need. Her mind, said to ignore, pretend, deflect.

Ciara smiled and continued. "It's not like the way I can work with the emotions. I've used that one most of my life without even knowing it."

Jada needed to push these growing feelings she had for Ky down, down, down. Her mind was right. She'd deflect all she could, shift the focus away from herself. "Fleur, I've seen your power over the plants. Can you use the other elements too?"

Maybe all dragon mates were white witches. Which meant Jada was not one. The human part of her had some light, but the rest of her was dark and black.

Not fit to be anyone's mate.

Fleur nodded. "My mother is a flower nymph, so most of what I can do is from her. But, when Steele and I mated—" she glanced over at her dragon warrior before continuing, "I met the White Witch too. She brought something more out in me."

Fleur stood took a deep breath. Every dragon warrior,

each mate, sat waiting, fixated, sensing something important was about to happen.

A shimmer washed over Fleur's body. The green dragon mark on her neck and collarbone stretched its wings.

Her eyes changed, her pupils elongating, the green in them more pronounced, stunning. Small sharp talons extended from her hands and white scales flicked across her skin.

She didn't shift fully into a dragon, but the shard at her neck glowed.

There were no such thing as female dragons. Leon had made that a point.

Jada stared along with everyone else. She wasn't as focused on Fleur's transformation, as the soul shard she wore. Ciara had one too. Neither of their dragons did.

A longing, beyond hunger, so deep inside of her, it had to come from her soul, struck her with the force of a tsunami. The dragons had given their mates their souls.

Steele stepped up and stood directly behind Fleur, his own dragon just below the surface, growling at the other dragon warriors, guarding, claiming his mate.

Ky, Dax, and Jakob didn't move. They weren't any threat to Fleur. They were surprised was all.

Ciara breathed out a sigh and helped the rest of them do the same. "Fleur. That's amazing. But, you might put it away before Steele drags you off to his lair."

Fleur blinked a few times and the scales and talons receded. Steele bent and whispered something in her ear that made her blush. A couple of daisies popped up from the floor under their feet.

"The White Witch is obviously trying to help us, but we've got to help ourselves with what she's given us." Not that Jada was sure how she could contribute unless Kur-Jara wanted to let her drink him dry.

She'd figure that out later. Another attack could come at any time, now that they knew the demon dragons could come out to play during the day.

"The dragons have their powers over the elements. Ciara, you can play with all four, along with a fifth element that includes emotions, Fleur has some serious flower power fueled by something unique, and I'm not sure how to help, but I've got my hypnotic allure. We have to be able to cobble all that together into a plan of some kind."

Ky smiled like a fool at her. "Don't forget your sexy smarts, *aroha*."

She hid the shiver his words gave her. "The question is, how can we harness those powers to keep everyone safe from Kur-Jara?"

"It sure would help if the rest of the dragons had badass mates too." They all looked over at Dax.

"Hey, hey, hey." Dax raised his hands holding back the stares of the ladies. "Don't look at me. I haven't even hit my Prime yet."

Fleur waggled her fingers at him. "You need a visit from the White Witch."

The front door blew open and Ninsy, in a flowing gown and a sword at her waist, walked into the room, appearing out of thin air.

Dax squeaked like a baby mouse and bolted for the kitchen.

Steele and Jakob shimmered into their dragon forms, blocking the room. Jada shot a look at Ky, but he shook his head.

Ninsy went right up to the green dragons and patted them

both on the noses. She spoke briefly to Jakob, but quietly enough that only the two of them could hear what she said. Then she squeezed between the two and plopped down onto an empty seat on the couch. She picked up the cup of coffee that Jada hadn't yet touched. "Got any donuts to go with this?"

Jada hugged her boss and badass fighter friend. "Ninsy, I thought you were dead. What happened to you?"

"Do you know this, umm, woman?" Fleur asked.

Ky stood and placed a hand on Ninsy's shoulder. "She helped us battle the demon dragons yesterday. She is a friend."

Ninsy lifted her cup in cheers to Ky. "Sorry about leaving you like that. I can't let the Black Dragon know of my existence in this world. I knew the two of you would get out of there alive and I left you the weapon I enchanted to destroy demon dragons. I'm glad you figured it out and used it."

"The rhubarb Danishes?"

Fleur held up one finger, pausing the reunion. "You used rhubarb to destroy demon dragons? That's what was all over Jada's clothes. It's so toxic, especially to lizards. Why didn't I think of that? I've got some growing in the community garden now."

She closed her eyes and held out both of her hands. Swirls of green ether flickered in her palms. "It's ready for harvest now. Nice big leaves and roots. Will you share the rest of your enchantment with us? And also, who are you?"

Ninsy smiled and nodded. "I've been sent by my mistress to help you in your upcoming battles with Kur-Jara."

Jakob and Steele shifted back and rejoined their mates. They both eyed Ninsy warily. Jada couldn't blame them, but maybe together the whole group could devise a way to get the Black Dragon and his minions off her tail and leave all the mates alone.

"Ninsy, do you know why the demon dragons and Kur-Jara are attacking me?"

Fleur sat next to Ninsy. "Or why he kidnapped me?"

Ninsy nodded and took another sip of her coffee. "For the same reason he wants the soul shards."

"Those bastards tried to take both mine and Steele's shards before we gave them to our mates. Ky have they attempted to get yours?"

"No, but, they may have another. Jakob?" Ky was asking a question only the two Wyverns understood.

Jakob nodded. "Cage Gylden's soul shard has been stolen." He turned his gaze on Jada. "By a succubus."

Aw, shit on a shingle.

Every eye in the place turned to Jada. All of them were asking if she'd done it. All except Ky's.

Was it possible to fall in love in one day with someone so different from herself in one day? She knew other shifters had fated mates, but they mostly mated their own kind, sometimes humans. Never demons

Could it be possible that she was Ky's true mate? Was that why she was feeling this way, all gooey inside like a custard-filled éclair?

That was it. The mates.

"I think Kur-Jara wants more than the shards. Whatever he's planning, he wants them and the mates. Together."

Ciara grasped for Jakob's hand. He gave it to her and pulled her to him. Steele did the same with Fleur.

Jada bit her lip. She didn't know what made her think she could ever have that instant support from anyone in her life. Just because Ky had claimed her didn't mean—

A hand slipped into hers and squeezed, interlacing their

fingers. Her eyes must have been as big as the moon when she looked over at him.

Ninsy bit into a donut and watched them all like they were the most interesting show on TV.

Hey, where'd she get a donut?

Dax edged his way back into the room. But, stayed as far as he could from Ninsy. "That's all well and fine, and by fine, I mean fucking horrible. So now we need a plan to protect the shards and every woman, witch, and succubus out there in case they are potential mates?"

"We can't protect the whole world from the demon dragons. No, I have a better idea." Jada lifted a hand when all four of the dragon warriors protested. "I'm not saying you haven't done a great job of that. But, that was before Kur-Jara decided to ante up."

"What do you suggest we do? Give up?" Dax folded his arms and glared. She couldn't blame him for being suspicious of her. She was a succubus after all.

"No. The opposite. I don't want you to protect us. I want you to let us join in the fight."

There were a whole lot of "hell no" and "you're crazy" were tossed at her. From everyone except Ky.

He joined her in the center of the group and faced Jakob first.

"Jakob. Who saved your ass when a horde of demon dragons buried you trying to get your soul shard?"

Jakob fixed his gaze on his mate. So much affection, and dare she name it — love —glowed out of him. "Ciara."

The shard at Ciara's neck glowed with its beautiful green and white light. She took Jakob's hand and squeezed.

Ky nodded and faced Steele, who glared back at him.

"Who smacked the Black Dragon upside the head with a tree and got herself out of the depths of hell?"

His glare turned into a pride-filled grin. "Fleur."

A daisy popped up in Steele's hair, and the light from around Fleur's throat joined with Ciara's.

"Who did the both of you give your soul shards to, full well knowing they would keep your souls safe while you went off to battle?"

Steele and Jakob stared into the eyes of their mates.

Jada's chest tightened, all the muscles around her heart and down to her stomach clenching. She wasn't sure whether her body was responding to the mushy-gooshiness of the people around her, so in love, a feeling she'd never thought she'd ever feel, or in anticipation of what she was sure Ky was going to say next.

"And who do you think saved my ass from a mountain of demon dragons and this Black Dragon himself? With only rhubarb filling for a weapon?"

He glanced from warrior to warrior.

Jada's muscles unclenched, and she let out a breath. She hasn't even realized she'd been holding it in.

"Yeah, that's right. Jada. So, I think it's only fair to hear what she has to say about our mates joining the fight."

Ky sat back down, but not before making a show of kissing Jada on the top of her head.

Warmth and tingles dripped down over her. There were too many fuzzy feels to take in. She pushed those to the back of her mind. Concentrate on the here and now and how to communicate her plan.

Sweet baby cheese-whiz. She hoped the inkling of an idea that had sparked sounded as good coming out of her mouth as it did in her head.

"Instead of protecting, which is an impossible task, we need to go on the offensive. Take the battle to the Black Dragon. Or rather, bring him to us."

Ky nodded, agreeing with her before he even knew what she had in mind. "How?"

Jada looked from Ciara to Fleur and back. They were both so powerful, and so precious to their mates. They were all about the girl power. They'd buy in, right?

She glanced over at Ky quickly. Hopefully none of them would want to kill her for what she was about to suggest.

They might. It was a brilliant and brilliantly stupid idea. One that could get them all killed. Or worse.

"Use us," she said, waving her hand in a triangle between herself and the other women, "as bait."

YOUR LOVE IS BETTER THAN DONUTS

No way, no how was Ky going to let Jada use herself as bait for the Black Dragon and his demon children. The thought of it had his own dragon roaring to get out.

The wise minded warrior part of him knew she had a solid idea and that it could work. He walked right into this, touting her smarts and skills. God, she was a badass.

Dammit.

He wanted to wrap her up in candy floss and hide her away from the world. She'd had enough fighting and strife from his enemies. A mate was for loving, protecting, kissing, and bedding. Not bait.

"Ky, quit shaking your head at me. You know this is the best chance of getting Kur-Jara off our backs." There was less demand and more vulnerability in Jada's voice. She wanted him to back her up.

That's what true mates did.

He hadn't even realized he'd been shaking his head at her. Ky unfolded his arms and quieted the dragon inside. If ever there was a time to show Jada he had every faith in her, this was it.

He did believe in her and her plan. It hurt to his core to think of her in danger, but he would tolerate any pain to ensure she knew she could count on him.

Ky glanced over at Steele and Jakob. Their dragons shimmered near the surface too, the tattoos stretching and writhing up their necks trying to free themselves. The men remained calm, their attention on Ky, waiting for his decision.

His mate, his choice.

He could very clearly see in the thrashing of the dragon tattoos that they hated the idea as much as he did. Maybe with a lot of time, a dozen more dragon warriors, and some super smarts, they could come up with a better plan.

They had none of those.

Ky would call upon the strength of the First Dragon to see him through this. He was afraid he wasn't strong enough on his own to see Jada and the other mates risk their lives.

He stared into Jada's eyes. There were flashes of uncertainty and hopefulness there. He would not let her down. He would not let her die. "You will not put yourselves in any kind of unnecessary danger."

Jada stood to protest, but Ky lifted a hand to stop her, just as she had to all of them. "It is a good idea. It scares the balls off me, but it could be our best option. Together, we can all figure out how to make it work, without putting the three of you in too much peril."

His mate tried to hide a smile by pressing her lips together. Soon, she would learn she never had to hide anything from him.

"Tell us your plan, *aroha.*"

Jada nodded and took a deep breath. "I've got two

scenarios in my head. One at night where we're all prepared for them and the other during the day, if they come to surprise us again."

"Demon dragons need the darkness and shadows to manifest. They aren't going to attack in the day."

"Kur-Jara grows bolder, stronger. I suspect with Ereshkigal's help." Ninsy dunked her cruller in her coffee.

Where had she gotten a donut?

"What does that mean?" Steele asked.

"Yesterday, we were attacked in daylight." First Ky had discovered demon dragons with gills, then they encountered the bastards in daylight. There was some powerful dark magic helping the Black Dragon and his army.

Steele took a step forward. "Holy shit. They could find us here at any time. Why haven't they attacked already?"

Ninsy pulled a sword from the sheath at her back and drew a symbol in the air with it. The air sparked and glowed with a silvery light in the shape of a protection ward. "The Black Dragon won't be able to find you for a few more hours at least."

Ciara stared at the glowing sigil and grinned at Ninsy. "Ooh. I've been doing research to better understand my powers. That's a protection ward. It should give us time to make a plan to get this guy."

Jakob put a possessive hand on Ciara's shoulder. "We'll call in all available dragon warriors to ensure our mates are not harmed. I know Match has some reds on the West Coast of America. Dax, can you contact them and tell them to get their asses over here?"

"Fuck yeah." Dax whipped out a phone from his pocket and walked back into the kitchen.

Ky wanted all the Wyverns here if they were going to

battle the Black Dragon. Their powers played off each other to make them stronger as a whole.

Cage was barely holding on to life, and Ky was still tasked with getting that shard back. He knew to his core, Jada hadn't stolen it. But, maybe she could find out who had.

"I agree. We all call in as much of our Wyrs as can get here in the next few hours. The Black Dragon's last attack was in daylight, so we cannot afford the luxury of waiting to gather until nightfall."

Jakob pulled out his phone too. "I don't have any more greens on this continent, but Cage may have some golds. I want to check on him anyway."

"Ninsy, will you help me with the rhubarb potion?" Fleur asked.

Ciara gave Jada's arm a quick squeeze before she stood up and followed the others toward the kitchen. "I'm hoping Ninsy will show us that sigil she drew. I'd like to add some more protection spells into my magical grab bag o'fun."

Ninsy nodded to Ciara. "As you wish, mistress."

That left just Steele, Jada, and Ky to build the plan. If Jada could contact her coven, they could add to the strength of the dragon warriors.

Her father's experience and knowledge of the Black Dragon would be invaluable, just as Jada's had been.

But could they be trusted? One of them had most likely stolen Cage's soul shard. Portia had mentioned being away. Nah. She didn't seem Cage's type.

Although, every woman was Cage's type.

An inkling of an idea to capture the Black Dragon and find Cage's shard at the same time formed in his mind. It would mean Jada betraying someone in her family.

He'd barely won a shred of her trust. He would win the

rest. He had to. Not just for Cage, or the fate of dragonkind, or to win this god-damned battle. But, he selfishly wanted her for his own. Wanted her trust and faith and loyalty all wrapped up in love.

Love?

With the depth of all the ocean, yes. He'd fallen head over tail for her the second he saw her cramming donuts into her mouth.

He'd buy her a hundred donuts shops if she'd love him back.

What the hell had the First Dragon and the White Witch done to him? How could he feel so deeply for a woman, one who was part demon, whom he'd only known existed a day ago?

He had to get his mind out of the mushy fluffy love nest it was building and get back to being a warrior.

"Jada, can we call upon your family again to help us?"

"If any of them besides Leon are still alive. But, I'd rather not have to summon him again. He really hates that." Jada shrugged. "But, I don't know how else to contact him. It's not like I have anyone's number. I didn't even know Portia had a phone. They've all hidden a lot from me."

There was both anger and hurt in her voice.

He was the dumbass about to hide more from her.

He couldn't ask for her trust when he didn't give his own. When the plans were set, and he had her alone, he'd tell her everything.

Ky took her hand in his and stroked the inside of her palm. She blinked at him, surprised, like he was doing something special.

He'd do a lot more special things to her when this was over. "Let's hash out this plan. I don't want to bring the Black

Dragon and his minions to your home, Steele. What about the area we fought in last time, when we battled for Fleur?"

Steele shook his head. "It is sacred to the other shifters in this area. I don't think they'd be very happy about another dragon battle in their backyard."

"We can be bait pretty much anywhere," Jada said.

Steele paced, glancing toward the kitchen and then back. "There has to be more to the plan than dangling the women. We need to surprise him."

Jada twisted one side of her mouth in an adorable thinking face. "That's as far as I got. We dangle, then when he shows up to nab us, we nab him instead."

Jakob rejoined them, Ciara in tow. "Can't get ahold of Match, but Cage has golds who can be here in a matter of hours. I've sent more greens to his place to protect him and heal what they can. He sounded like shit."

The sooner they could capture the Black Dragon, the sooner he could hunt down Cage's shard. "Jada, would one of your kind work with the Black Dragon to get him that shard?"

She shook her head. "I don't know why they would. He'd have to have a pretty compelling reason and the succubus would have to hide what she was doing from her coven. I always thought it was hard to hide anything from one's demon family, but I guess I was wrong about that."

"How did the succubus who took Cage's shard get him to give it up to her?" Ky asked her.

"I don't know." Jada tapped a finger to her lips. "What would make a dragon warrior give his shard to anyone?"

They looked at Steele and Jakob. "You're the only two dragons who ever have. Why did you give your mates your shard?"

"It wasn't my shard I was giving Fleur. It was my soul."

That only confirmed what Ky had been feeling. He didn't know if Jada would want it, but his soul reached for her, wanted him to give her a part of himself.

Ciara and Jakob exchanged a meaningful look and clasped hands. "I was dying. I thought if I gave it to her, she would still have a part of me and could keep it safe from the demon dragons."

"How did you know it was the right thing to do, to give it to them?" Ky should be focused on defeating the Black Dragon. His mind pushed everything else aside, except for whether he should give his own shard to Jada.

"If a succubus was able to get the shard from a Wyvern in the first place, it should be a piece of cake for Jada to get it from the Black Dragon."

Steele shook his head. "But he has the crone. She's got some scary powerful magic according to Fleur. What if Jada can't?"

Jada rubbed her forehead. "There isn't much that can defend against a succubus's allure when she turns it on full throttle, but—"

"Then why don't we just have Jada use her power on the Black Dragon anyway and have her compel him to give up?"

"It doesn't work that way. It's a short burst, that makes someone horny enough to want to please me, you know, sexually. I can't force them to do anything."

"Have you ever used it for anything else?" Ciara asked.

"Well, no. I guess I never needed to."

Ciara rubbed her hands together. "Try it out on us. We're already mated, so I don't think it will affect us."

Jada sunk back. "No. I,…no. That's not a good idea."

Ciara was perky and bright. It was hard to tell her no. "It

will be fine. We need to see if it can help. See if you can get us to do something we wouldn't normally do."

"I don't like this."

Ky didn't either. If need be, he would defend his mate against any other dragon on the face of the planet. Even his own fellow Wyverns, his brotherhood.

The other women returned from the kitchen. Fleur said, "We have to go to the community garden to get the rhubarb. I only have stalks and the leaves and roots are the most toxic."

Ky nodded to her. "Steele and Dax will take you. But first, we're going to try a little experiment. We can see if she has a different effect on mated versus unmated dragons."

He hated how uncomfortable this made Jada, but Ciara was right. He lifted her hand to his lips and kissed the inside of her wrist, drawing her attention away from the other dragons and their mates.

"This could be a powerful weapon. I know you don't want to, but I promise to protect you if anything goes wrong."

Jada chewed on her lip, worrying the skin there. "This is still a bad idea, but I'll try."

"Thank you."

"Get Dax in here."

"Wait. See if Jada can get him with her allure."

Jada rolled her eyes and shook her head. "I hope he's got a girlfriend."

"I'll throw him in the fountain if can't keep his cool."

Jada nodded and closed her eyes, concentrating as if in a quiet meditation. When she opened them, her pupils had gone from normal sized to full blown, making her eyes look completely black. She tipped her head and aimed her forehead at the hallway to the kitchen.

Metal clanged to the floor, and Fleur winced but didn't say

anything. In fact, no one said a word. They were all focused completely on Jada.

Dax stalked into the living room, as if he was hunting prey. That prey was Jada. He growled low and deep at Ky. "Get away from her, Puru. She's mine."

Jada moved so Ky's body blocked hers. "I told you this was a bad idea."

Ky stood and hovered in front of Jada breaking Dax's path and sight. His dragon rippled across his skin, wanting to protect its mate. "Can you turn it off?"

Jada blinked. "I already have, but the power of the allure lasts for hours."

Talons extended from Dax's hands and red scales shimmered across his skin. Smoke poured from his nostrils.

"Oh, crap. He's going to light our house on fire." Fleur moaned.

"Jada. Don't push it down. Turn your allure on him full force, but tell him what you want from him." Ninsy's voice was low.

"If I use the full power, everyone else will be affected too." Jada shook her head, everything in her body language screamed 'no way.'

Ninsy wasn't fazed. "Probably, but you can control the situation."

Fleur tipped her head to the side, as if trying to remember something. "Wait, how much of your power did you already use on him?"

"Maybe ten percent. I rarely need much more than that."

"I felt this last night. I thought my hormones were out of whack. But it was you, wasn't it?"

Jada nodded at Fleur. "Sorry about that. It sort of slipped out. Moment of weakness."

Ninsy interrupted again. "Use it all, Jada. Let go."

Jada sighed and addressed the other women. "Please, take ahold of your dragons' hands, or sit on their laps or something. I don't know what's going to happen."

Both women scrambled to do as she requested. Dax lurked closer, never taking his eyes off Ky.

He'd put Dax on ice before he allowed the red dragon to touch his mate.

Jada slipped her hand into Ky's. She vibrated with power, sending a warm glow through him. His own shard lit up, and Dax glared at it and him.

Ninsy's voice was quiet but commanding, like a yogi guiding new initiates to the path of consciousness. "Now, Jada. You can do this. Open your heart and your mind."

Jada sucked in a long breath and held it for a count of three. Then the room filled with a pulsing energy so intense Ky's cock pushed at his pants, going from ready to harder than stone in an instant. Every dragon in the room sported tents in their pants, and there was no hiding it.

Dax fell to his knees, then all fours. He roared, flames licking at his lips, but he fought the shift and his dragon stayed contained.

Jada slowly blinked and turned her gaze on Ky. He almost came right there in his pants like a randy teenaged dragon chasing his first woman.

"Holy Mother Earth," Fleur whispered. She sat on Steele's knee and looked at his lap like her eyes had no other place in the room to go.

Ciara's eyes went wide, and she yanked her mate up from his chair and began dragging him away.

"Excuse us, please. I need to, we are...we'll be right back. In about three hours."

Jada slumped into her chair. "Ah hell. See. I told you this is what would happen. It's just sex."

"Ciara, wait. Command them, Jada. Ask them to do what you want from them." Ninsy lifted her chin indicating the circle of people around them.

Ky was ready to rip Jada's clothes off and take her right there on the carpet. Ninsy only looked mildly interested in what Jada was doing, but nothing else. She didn't seem to be having any response to Jada's powers at all.

"What do you mean?"

"Try it, mistress. See what happens."

"What do I say?"

"You decide. But, do it quickly. When you use this much power, your allure burns out much quicker. It is already beginning to fade."

So, she did feel it, but it didn't do anything to her. Dax on the other hand looked ready to pounce., every muscle tensed, his gaze still wholly focused on Jada.

"Umm. Okay, here goes. Don't kill me for this. It's the only thing I could think of. Everybody do the chicken dance."

Ky found his arms folding, and his thumbs tucked themselves up under his armpits. Then he started flapping his elbows.

Dax moved to his feet and did the same. "What the fuck is going on?"

Ciara and Fleur burst into laughter, but neither Jakob nor Steele joined in the dance.

"Ladies," Ninsy said, holding out her hand "ask your mates to do the same, if you would please."

Ciara sighed, but spoke into her mate's ear. His eyes narrowed at her, but she whispered something else and his look turned to lust.

He flapped his arms in the same way as Ky.

"Chicken it up, my love," Fleur instructed Steele.

He scowled but joined the other men.

Ciara giggled. "This could be very handy. Jada, wouldn't you like to come on an extended visit to the Czech Republic? We have a lovely guest house on our property.

Jakob scowled at Ciara making promises with his eyes and flapping chicken wings. "Does this work the other way around?"

"Find out for yourselves," Ninsy said.

Steele's scowl turned into a grin. "Come here and give me a good long kiss, my flower."

"You don't have to compel me to do that." Fleur's shard glowed, and she kissed Steele long and hard. One little, two little, three little flowers popped up in her hair. "I have a lot more things in mind, but they aren't appropriate in front of our company."

Steele waggled his eyebrows at his mate. "You don't have to make me do any of what is on your dirty mind either. I'll happily fulfill all those fantasies later."

Jakob whispered something in Ciara's ear, and she instantly flapped her arms in the air like the men. Her cheeks also flushed much deeper than what the little bit of exertion called for.

The shard at her neck sparkled too.

"Are we done with your little game? My arms are getting tired." Dax huffed, but there was still lust in his eyes when he looked at Jada.

Her jaw hung open. "Oh. Sorry. Yeah. Umm. At ease."

Ky's arms fell to his side and the vibrating power he'd felt before lifted. He still had a throbbing hard on and a need to take Jada in every way possible.

Jada blew out a long breath and took hold of Ky's hand again. "That was exhausting."

He ran a hand over her head and through her hair, then pulled her up and kissed her quickly but with a lick and a promise for more to come later "And amazing. Still think you can't make the Black Dragon do what you want?"

He knew she could. With that power the second Jada opened her mouth he would fly to the moon and back if she asked him too. It was more than a little disconcerting that Dax was under her influence too.

Jakob nodded. "If he's already got the shard, we won't be able to take it from him. But, with Jada's power—"

Yep. That was exactly what Ky had been thinking. Jada was their secret weapon.

"I could." She smiled up at him, yawned and then collapsed into his arms.

"Oh god. Is she okay?" Fleur rushed over.

Her breathing came deep and even, but Ky looked to Fleur and Ninsy to see if they could help.

Ninsy touched Jada's forehead. "She'll be fine as long as Ky feeds her and takes care of her needs."

He'd do that and more.

Jada's eyelids fluttered, and Ky noticed her fangs had extended. The shower was not going to cut it this time. He needed to claim her, take her long and hard, and make her come at least half a dozen times.

JUST GETTING STARTED

Jada struggled to get back to consciousness. The bloodlust she'd left behind last night when Ky fed and cared for her came back with a force worse than before.

Would he want to feed her again?

She couldn't yet pry her eyes open, but she could hear the voices of the people she'd controlled with her allure all around her.

Controlled. The thought turned her insides into jam filling. Sickly sweet. Like her first taste of blood.

So good, and so bad.

Could all her brothers and sisters use their allure like that? Could Leon?

If they could, why didn't they?

Or maybe they did. One more secret they'd kept from her.

"We'd all better have a short break and take care of our... needs."

That was Ciara. She'd definitely felt Jada's power, but hadn't been directly controlled by it.

Jada slid one eye open a tiny slit and found Dax's gaze fixed right on her.

"You fuckers. What am I supposed to do?" Dax stared longingly at her but kept his distance and waved his hand in front of his pants.

Shoot. That really wasn't fair. She had no doubts at all that everyone else was about to go have noisy, very satisfying sex, and poor Dax had no one.

She closed her eyes again and figured a hot shifter like him could probably pick up a girl no problem.

"We've got about an hour before the golds show up. I suggest a nice cold shower."

"God damn it." Dax stomped off toward the front door.

"Ninsy, will your ward hold out for a little while longer? I still want to get that rhubarb, but there's one or two things I need to do first." Fleur made bedroom eyes at Steele.

"Those things you need to do better be me." Steele's voice was filled with a need he was trying his best to keep under control.

"They are," Fleur said.

"Yes, you are all safe for now." Thank goodness for Ninsy.

But what in the world was Ninsy that she'd known that Jada had that kind of power when Jada didn't know herself?

"Go, play with your mates now. You'll need the power you can get from the coupling in the battles to come."

Jada had always known there was power in sex, but was it true for other beings too? Had Ky gotten as much from her last night as she had from him?

She yawned and finally pried both eyes open. Ky stared down at her. She was in his arms.

That made all the warm fuzzies attack her heart. Silly.

Ciara grabbed Jakob's hand. "Hey Fleur, you don't happen to have any haystacks in your yard, do you?"

Fleur giggled. "No, but give me a minute and I can grow you two a nice secluded field of wheat. I think you'll like that even more."

"Hurry it up, little flower, because that mud bath is calling our names. An hour isn't nearly long enough for what I want to do to you."

Fleur shivered, raised her hands and within a minute little sprouts made a path out the door. "Follow those and you'll find your field.

"Oh, and Ky. There's hot springs on the far side of the property I think you'll enjoy." Fleur winked and grabbed Steele's hand dragging him out of the room.

Jada moved to get up, but Ky lifted her and carried her out the door, shifting in a flash to his dragon form, wrapping her gently in his great claws.

"*Are you all right,* aroha? *I was worried.*"

"I'm mostly fine. Hungry though."

"*Good. I'll feed you.*"

"I mean, hungry for—"

"*I will feed you in every way that you need.*"

He landed a moment later, setting her on the ground before shifting back to his human form. But this time he didn't have on the clothes he'd been wearing before.

He wasn't wearing anything at all.

Gods above and below, he was so damn good looking it made her lower belly clench just at the sight of him.

The tattoos and scars across his dark body so different from her unmarred pale skin. Except she wasn't unmarred. She had a blue dragon mark on her neck and shoulder.

"You're staring, sweet thing."

The last time she'd seen him naked, she hadn't taken the time to really get a good look at him. She'd been too desperate for what he offered. Sex and blood. "Yeah. And I'm gonna keep staring. Are all dragon warriors so yummy?"

His eyes twinkled. "Nope. Only me."

Only him, for only her.

That was too weird. She knew most non-humans mated for life, and she'd heard stories of fate intervening, of true mates. Those tales never involved a succubus. Mates weren't important to demons. Family and the coven provided all the companionship and support any demon needed.

This pull she felt, down to her black soul, couldn't be ignored. She not only needed him, she wanted to be with him. It hurt to even think of not having him in her life.

She never believed she'd ever have anyone in her life like that. Ky saw something in her that she didn't see herself. She didn't feel quite so dark and lonely inside when she was with him.

Ky prowled around her, circling, looking her up and down. He came up behind her, licked the side of her neck and ran a hand into her hair. "What's going on inside that beautiful brain of yours, Jada?"

She wished she had a one-track mind at the moment. She'd pick the get-down-and-dirty-with-Ky train. "Too many things."

"Like what?"

Like about a million trillion reasons why a hot alpha male like Ky would ever want to be with a chubby little succubus at all. And how soon he'd realize that despite the mating spell he seemed to be under.

Probably as soon as this battle with the Black Dragon was over and he saw how she didn't have a clue what she was doing. He'd send her packing right back to Leon and her coven. Back to her insipid life, eating savorless meals that did nothing more than sustain her life.

"I was thinking about exactly how delicious you are." That wasn't a lie. His blood, his sex, made her mouth water simply thinking about how utterly naked he was, pressed against her back, his cock already hard against her butt.

"Hmm. I think there's more going on than that, but, I'll take it. Especially since that's what I was thinking about." His tongue ran across a spot behind her ear that made her knees go all wobbly.

"And I've been waiting hours to taste this part of you too." He nipped her earlobe and sucked it into his mouth, flicking the tip of his tongue over the skin.

Hells bells. Who knew her earlobes had direct zip-zing access between her legs? Apparently sexy dragon warriors, because Ky reached across her thighs and pushed the skirt of her dress up.

The only piece of clothing Fleur hadn't had any unworn spares to lend her was panties. Jada's hot skin was bare to the world.

"Holy fuck, doll. If I'd known you didn't have anything on under this dress all morning, I might have told the rest of the group to figure out their own god-damned plan to battle the Black Dragon. Because I'd be spending my time and efforts on licking your sweet pussy until you screamed my name."

That's what she was afraid of. This kind of sex was still so new to her, and she didn't want Ky to think she was a cold fish. What if she couldn't come again from his mouth on her sex?

"What if I want to lick you until you scream my name,

dragon?" That should do it. She knew how to give head. That was easy.

Letting go like she had last night, not so much. She didn't even know if she could do it again. Probably not.

He'd caught her in a moment of vulnerability when she'd been desperate and needy. She was hungry now, but not like before.

"I can hardly wait to see those red lips of yours wrapped around my cock. I'd love to fuck your mouth, let your sexy as hell fangs run across my shaft, teasing me with them and their touch of pain."

Yeah. She could do that. No problem. She'd get him off and slake the hunger with his energy.

No need for him to try and give her another orgasm. Even if it did fulfill her in a whole other way that was so much more satisfying.

It would be fine.

Ky stroked his fingers through the wisp of her curls. "We've got less than an hour, and you're already hot and wet. Come over to the water's edge and let me eat you, make you come in my mouth. Then you can have your fill of my blood."

Ky wrapped his arms around her and unbuttoned the top half of the dress. Her breasts ached for him to touch, caress, and fondle them.

Would he suck on them if she asked him to? Asking felt weird. Of course he would, but she needed to concentrate on what turned him on. But the low husky growl that came from his throat as he pushed the dress down around her shoulders was so deliciously distracting.

He deftly unhooked the plain tan bra and pushed it down her arms too so that her breasts were freed.

He cupped them in his hands and circled her nipples with his rough fingers until they were sensitive and hard.

The scruff of his unshaven face rubbed across her shoulder and the tender skin where he'd marked her. He looked down to where his hands were massaging her.

"Look how perfectly these fill my hands. My cock is going to look fucking amazing sliding between them later. After I spend a good long time seeing if I can make you come from sucking on your plump nipples."

There was no use trying to concentrate when her brain was frying from the heat of his touch and his words.

He gave her a little pinch, pushed the dress down her hips and dragged her to the edge of the spring, wading in.

She finally found her voice from where it was buried deep inside her own lust. This was not how she wanted this to go. He was the one who needed to come this time, not her. "No, wait."

She didn't step into the water and tried to pull him back. He didn't budge. "Would you rather I fucked you with my fingers while you feed from me?"

"No, I mean, yes, that sounds really great. Like almost as good as..." She shook her head, trying to get her own pleasure out of her head. "But, it's my turn to—"

"*Aroha*, I promise you, we will spend plenty of time in each other's bodies. I want you to ride me until neither of us can see straight. I plan to take you in every way I possibly can. Your mouth, your hot cunt, and you better believe I'm going to take that sweet ass of yours."

Well, when he put it that way, it made her want him even more.

"We'll do all that and more when we have the luxury of a private beach and a lot of undisturbed hours. If I start fucking you now, I won't be able to stop, and I won't put you at risk that way. Not when the Black Dragon could strike at any time."

"Not even if I do this?" Ninsy said we have at least an hour." Jada opened her allure and wrapped it around Ky. It had a new feeling about it, just as powerful, but not as dark, more sweet and sensual, rather than dominant need.

His breathing increased, and a drop of pre-cum pearled at the tip of his cock. But the only move he made was to raise an eyebrow at her.

"Jada." Her name was a low grumble, chastising even. "I plan on spending a lot longer than that fucking you."

Huh. He'd been affected by her allure a few minutes ago, but then Ninsy had her turn it on full blast. She opened herself more, letting the power flow out of her straight at Ky.

It wasn't fair of her, but she would not have him feed her with his body and blood and have nothing for himself. If she had to manipulate him with her finely honed succubus powers to do that, she would.

Ky blinked and incredibly, his eyebrow went up another degree. The muscles in his legs flex and his cock get even bigger. But, he didn't move to jump her bones as she expected.

Maybe he was waiting for her to command him like the chicken dance thing. "Come over here so I can touch you."

Ky slowly splashed out of the water, walked right up to her, and grabbed her head, pulling her in for a brutal kiss.

Their mouths smashed together, teeth and fangs clacking, his tongue penetrating her, thrusting in and out until she couldn't breathe.

He broke the kiss with a nip to her lip and tugged her head back by her hair, exposing her throat and chest. "Is this what you want, *aroha*? For me to take you, and fuck you, and claim you all over again?"

Ky scraped his teeth across the dragon on her collarbone, tugging at the skin. "Because I will do that whether you turn your sensuality on me like that or not."

Heat rushed across her face and neck, her heart pounding hard to fill the new needs of her body. What she wanted was to give Ky as much as he'd given her, to please him, to make his body sing for her.

But, oh, how her skin buzzed, and her veins pulsated in places she never knew it could when he took control like this.

"I. Want… Your. Cock." She forced the words out, opening her allure wider, turning it up another notch, beyond any level she'd ever used before.

He took one of her hands and dragged it down between their bodies and wrapped her fingers around his erection. "I cannot resist your commands. You've proven that. But, I will make them work for both of us."

He surrounded her hand in his, creating a double fist around his cock, and moved their fingers up and down his shaft.

He was thick and hard in her hand and she wanted to feel him pushing into her, taking her.

"Ky, fuck me. I want your cock inside of me."

He groaned and lowered his mouth to her neck again, thrusting into their fists. His teeth dug into her flesh, shooting pleasure pain through her until she felt the moisture between her legs.

She bowed under his bite, losing her equilibrium, betrayed by her own body's reaction to his total hold on her.

He seized her moment of weakness to pick her up and carry her into the water. "I want to give you soft, gentle loving, but if you need me to be dominant and rough, forcing the pleasure out of you so you can let go, I will make you submit to me."

She couldn't even admit that to herself. She wouldn't have to if she pushed him to the edge. Jada unlocked the final portion of the power she held inside and unleashed it on Ky.

"Make me."

Scales rippled across his skin, and the blue and bone talisman at his neck burst with light. The beautiful blue irises of his eyes elongated, and his dragon eyes stared down at her.

The dragon had come out to claim her, make her his.

This was what she needed more than anything else. Only with Ky could she open herself, show her true powers and know that he would give her everything and be able to take from her too.

She couldn't hurt him, so she could trust him to take care of her, like no one else ever could.

Ky strode back into the water, waist deep, and pushed her down against the nearest ledge, face first, forcing her hands over her head.

He covered her body with his, holding her down so she couldn't move, only take what he wanted from her. He notched his cock between her legs, pushing it through her folds, not entering her, but scraping the head across her sensitive clit.

She moaned and wriggled against him. She needed him inside of her. Now. "Ky."

He used his hips to press her harder against the rock, water sloshing over them, pinning her body beneath his until she stilled.

"Good girl." He withdrew and shoved into her again, using his cock like an erotic toy. He moved in short thrusts, rubbing her clit with the head over and over. He growled into her ear. "Is this what you need, my love?"

Jada couldn't move, couldn't reply, could hardly breathe. The power of the allure flowed over and through her to Ky and back again. She could feel his desire as deeply as her own.

He wanted her so completely, but not in the way her victims had. He wasn't there only for himself. His pleasure was hers and he took it from her, returning it tenfold.

He gave the sexual energy to her willingly so that she didn't need to suck it from him, No longer stealing, taking, feeling like it would never be enough. That alone gave her the freedom she needed to lose herself in the pleasure, and finally let go.

Jada's legs shook, and she gasped for air. "Yes. Please, Ky."

"That's right baby, let go. Come for me."

He released of one of her arms and she didn't move it from the spot he'd held it down. His fingers dug into her back and then her hip as he worked his way down her body. "Fuck your body is beautiful like this, submitting to me."

His thrusts across her clit turned even shorter and faster and then suddenly his fingers were there too, sliding across her when his cock withdrew.

"Come Jada, let me see you explode for me."

Supernovas ignited before her eyes, and her body detonated into uncontrollable shudders, the orgasm flowing across her whole body.

Ky continued to circle her clit with his fingers, drawing more ripples of pleasure out of her in ongoing tremors from her core.

When her body shuddered for the last time, Ky pulled her up and turned her, taking her into his arms.

He wasn't gentle with her even now. The first thing he did

was give her another brutal kiss while lifting her legs, so she straddled him.

She wanted to lay her head on his shoulder and ride the high from the sex energy, the orgasm, and his total domination of her.

"I told you once I fucked you, I wasn't going to be able to stop, unless you say no. We're just getting started."

TAKE MY SOUL

*K*y had been with more than his fair share of beautiful sexy women in his life. Young dragons were horny bastards. He'd never had his brains fucked out so thoroughly without even being inside his partner.

His cock ached from wanting to be in Jada, thrusting as deep as he could. Selfish fucker.

Jada needed him to be better than that. More than a splash in the water. No, he would win her heart and soul by being more than a lover.

If Ky wanted Jada to give him everything he needed to give her all of himself.

Her body still vibrated with the after effects of her orgasm, and there was no way he was letting her come down from that high. He wanted to push her over the edge again and again and again.

He happened to know firsthand that she'd never experienced multiple orgasms. It was time to correct that oversight.

He waded deeper into the spring until they were both

submerged past their waists. "Wrap your legs around me and sink your tight pussy down on my cock."

Being in the water like this made it easier for him to maneuver, and he only needed one hand to support her back. He reached between them and grabbed his cock, groaning at even that much friction. She had him harder than he could ever remember being. There was no way he'd last very long inside her wet heat. But, he also had the feeling that with the power of her allure, he'd be ready to go again before they even got their breath back.

She was his own personal Viagra-athon.

Jada held his hips with her thighs and slowly sank down. He positioned his cock right at her entrance and then slipped his hand out, so she could sheath him.

Holy Ranginui and all the Māori gods, being inside of her was a goddamn spiritual event. She was heaven, Nirvana.

She gripped his arms, digging her nails in reflexively. "Ky, oh, Ky. You feel so good inside of me."

"It's gonna feel even better when you ride me." He grabbed her hips, sinking his fingers into the soft flesh and moved her down, so he was fully seated inside of her. Oh yeah. He could stay right here for the rest of his life.

But there were those multiple orgasms to get to.

He pushed against her hips, sliding her off his dick, and then slammed her back down. He did that over and over, showing her how to move, until she understood and rode him of her own accord.

"That's it, good girl. Fuck me, Jada. Fuck me."

She panted. "Tell me if I'm not doing it right."

Shit, he'd forgotten his promise to help her let go by making sure she didn't have to control the pleasure. He'd actually been thinking she would be able to come easier if she was in control. But, that wasn't his Jada. That was other women… And for him there were no longer any other women.

"My love, you've got me so turned on that you could make faces at me, and it would feel good. Stick out your tongue and I just might come right now."

Jada stilled. It wasn't exactly the most romantic thing to say.

"My love?"

Yes, he had said that. Was he ready to admit to her that he was in love with her? Was she ready to hear it?

Probably not. He would tell her soon though. For now, he would gloss over it. He smiled at her and brushed a light kiss across her lips for his answer to her question.

"Lay back in the water. I'll help you float. I want to see those gorgeous tits of yours bobbing on the surface."

She gave him a sideways look that said she knew what he was doing, but that she was going to go with it for now. She arched her back and splayed her arms out, laying herself down like the water was a fine featherbed. Her head tipped back, and her waves of black hair spread over the surface.

Ky controlled the water so that it didn't splash her in the face. Then he rocked his own hips, burying himself in her once again.

She closed her eyes and took him, all of him. He was buried so deep inside of her, he wasn't sure where he stopped and she began. The faster he thrust, the closer they got to becoming one.

That's what he wanted more than anything else in the world. For them to be as one. Nothing between them, only love.

He squeezed the globes of her ass under the water, keeping

a tight hold on her, slamming into her now. Her breasts jerked with each thrust as if he were fucking her tits too. He was this close to losing control and she wasn't yet ready to come.

"Put your fingers into your cunt and stroke your clit. Make yourself come for me. I want to see it. I need to see it."

There he was, being that selfish bastard. He should be giving her everything, taking care of her. He'd tried.

Someday, when he wasn't so frantic for her and her body, he'd make it up to her.

Jada put a hand between her legs, at first only covering up her mound. Ky already knew every inch of her intimately, she couldn't hide anything from him, certainly not her arousal.

"Spread your pussy lips. Show me your clit. Show me how hot and engorged it is for me."

She was so pink and so perfect down there, he could hardly wait to spend long leisurely hours just staring at her cunt. Then he would take another couple hours watching his cock slide in and out of her.

"Don't deny me what I want, Jada. Do what I said. Stroke yourself. I want to see your pussy clench when you come."

Jada had been silent since he said the L word, but with the first tentative stroke of her fingers he matched it with a thrust of his cock, and she groaned low and deep.

"Yes, baby. That's fucking beautiful. More." Ky's voice came out deep and husky. He had to grit his teeth to keep from exploding while watching her pleasure herself and seeing his cock slide in and out of her.

If she hadn't had an orgasm, he doubted she masturbated. From here on out she would be making up for lost time on that front. If he had his way, she'd make herself come while he watched at least twice a day.

He loved this shy virginal side of her. It made him feel like he was the only man she'd ever been with. By the time they made their mating official, he would have fucked her and made her come so much, she' forget anyone else she'd ever had sex with.

Her shy swipes across her clit became more confident as she figured out what felt good to her.

He knew she wasn't comfortable doing this for him, and he would dominate her again, take away her worries by making them his own. Right now, he wanted her to understand her own pleasure, her own body.

"Ky, it's too much. I…I'm coming."

"Yes, my love, come on my cock. Let me see it, feel it."

He wanted to feel her pussy walls clench down on him, and see those spasms shake her clit, but she lifted her head and stared into his eyes as she came, and he couldn't look away. They connected, with his soul touching hers. Her precious heart was open and out for him, all of her feelings and emotions in her eyes. He'd never seen anything more erotic and more gorgeous, ever.

His own orgasm slammed into him, and he jerked, his muscles taking over as he lost his rhythm and poured his seed into her.

"Fuck, Jada. I love you."

They were both silent for long minutes after it was over. Jada floated in the water, and Ky slipped from her thighs and drifted next to her, letting the water wash over them both. Looking for some peace.

"Ky?"

"Yeah, baby?"

"Do you?"

He wasn't going to pretend he didn't know what she was asking. He could play this all nonchalant, stare up at the sky and tell her he loved her. Not seeing her reaction to the words, hiding his own hurt.

He was no god-damned coward.

He stood again and pulled her into his arms. He used his power over the element to push them back to shore and laid her in the tall grass, only the water lapping at their feet.

Their lovemaking in the water hadn't been anything like he'd expected. He'd needed her so badly that it might have been nothing more than rough fucking.

It had been, was, so much more.

The muscles in Ky's chest squeezed, trying to protect his heart. He kept his life in order, served and protected the world from evil and plague. He could do that because he didn't allow himself to care about anyone or anything else. Not getting close to a woman, helped him do his job.

He had one purpose on this earth, and the gods, or the First Dragon, or maybe his own forsaken soul had decided a long time ago he would never have a true mate.

Fine. Didn't matter. He was happy as he was.

Until her. Jada changed everything.

Ky swallowed the namby-pamby rush of anxiety swirling in his throat and searched for the right words.

"Jada. I know it's too soon. We've only just met, but that doesn't matter to me. I am in love with you. You're smart, fearless when it counts, and vulnerable when you don't want to be, but need to be. You're gorgeous and funny, and I'm not sure how I would ever not be in love with you."

He ripped the soul shard from his neck and pressed it to her skin, not because he was supposed to, but because she already owned his soul. "Take me, *aroha*. Take all of me. You have my heart, my mind, and my body already. Take my soul and make it your own."

She clasped her hand over his and stilled, pain written on her face. "I have nothing to give you in return. I am nothing."

He wrapped his hand around the back of her neck making sure she couldn't look away. Searching for that connection he'd seen in her eyes. "You are everything. I wish you could see yourself through my eyes. I swear to you I will do everything in my power to make you feel how special and important you are to me."

She shook her head but didn't break his gaze.

"Give me your love, your trust, Jada. What you are is enough. Always."

She swallowed, and her eyes shimmered with tears. "I didn't mean to...I didn't know I needed you, that there was this empty part of me, until you showed up. You already have my love, Ky Puru. I think I fell in love with you somewhere between the moment I saw you in the donut shop and that very first kiss. How can that be?"

"It's fate. Because that's when I fell in love with you too. The rest has been candy on top."

She reached up and tied the torn edges of the cord around her neck. The blue shard settled between her breasts and a powerful wave of energy and blue light filled him to overflowing. He gripped Jada tight in his arms and she held him just as hard.

The power and light ebbed, and they were left holding each other, gasping for breath.

"Whoa. I feel like we've just ridden a roller coaster while drinking energy shots and having mind-blowing sex," Jada whispered.

He laughed. "Didn't we? Because, yeah. That pretty much describes that exact feeling."

Ky took a quick mental inventory of himself. A new layer

to his power, his affinity with the water pulsed through him. Nothing and everything seemed to have changed.

Once again, his cock was rock hard for her. He would never get enough. He kissed Jada, slipping his tongue in and out of her mouth, soft and slow. Their frantic fucking was fantastic, but he wanted to make intense, passionate, love to her now.

He lifted her leg and slipped it over his hip, opening her to him.

Her body was ready for him and he pushed his way into her pussy, filling her, making her his once again.

Jada laced her fingers into his hair and dipped her head to his neck. In the same spot he'd marked her, she bit his skin, sucking his blood into her mouth.

The euphoria of her bite hit Ky, and he suddenly knew he was feeling what she felt, and she was experiencing everything he experienced.

She was shocked at the depths of his feelings for her, how he saw the beauty and strength in her where she did not. Ky was equally shaken by the fierceness of that spark of love inside of her for him. A few hours ago, he was sure he was only barely tolerable to her.

She hid from love the same way he did.

If you didn't love anything, nothing mattered, and if it didn't matter, it didn't hurt if you lost it, or never found it in the first place.

But they had found each other.

Ky rocked into her body, needing to show her with every part of his being how much she meant to him, how much she mattered.

Their mouths met for long, deep kisses. Their hands and fingers roamed each other's bodies, until they were wrapped so tightly in each other that they were overwhelmed with bliss.

They stared into each other's eyes, sharing every pleasure and emotion their lovemaking drew out. This time when Jada came and her eyes locked on his, their souls twined together along with their bodies. He held nothing back.

"I love you, Jada. To the depths of the ocean and back, I love you."

He came inside of her again, feeling her body pulse around him, loving how deeply connected they were in this shared moment.

He didn't want to move, to leave her body. The way she grabbed his ass told him she didn't want him to either.

With her head laying in the grass he had access to her neck and stroked his fingers languidly across her blue dragon mark. Never had he felt such an intense level of...pure contentment.

Something scratched at his blissful state of mind, but he brushed it away. He wouldn't let anything interrupt this time with Jada.

"Enjoy fucking your whore, you blue bastard. It's the last pleasure you'll ever feel."

Nothing, except the devil himself.

ALLURE AND OTHER NATURAL DISASTERS

*J*ada's senses were overwhelmed with the dark and evil presence that surrounded her and Ky. One minute she was full of light and bliss, sure for the first time that the glimmer of light that had always been inside of her was stronger than the darkness. Ky's touch, his absolute belief that she was his true mate, and the power of the love that he felt for her took away all her fears, cravings, and insecurities.

The blackness of Kur-Jara's soul pushed out into everything around him. He was like a black hole but in reverse. It took everything she had inside to guard the growing ember of good Ky saw in her. She hid this new beautiful and pure part of her behind the brilliant blue light of his soul shard. The one he had given to her freely.

Ky rolled away from her and onto all fours. Within a breath he shifted into a great blue dragon. Water shot up from the hot spring and blasted their enemy.

Kur-Jara met Ky's attack with a blast of fire and smoke that evaporated the water before it hit him.

Her Ky wasn't dumb though. He used the second of time it took the black Dragon to defend himself to rain icicles of death down on Kur-Jara's black head.

The Black Dragon shrieked in pain as the ice sliced his scales from his body. Even his blood was black, turning to ash as it dropped from his skin.

Jada had been dumbstruck by the sneak attack, but no more. The plan to use her and the other mates as bait was shot to hell. However, she could still use the one weapon she had against him.

Ky's lovemaking and his declaration of love had replenished her, and she had energy to spare. She would need every bit of it to make her allure strong enough to affect the Black Dragon.

Jada centered herself remembering her very first lessons from Leon on how to bring her allure to the surface. She was used to only releasing a smidgen of it. Only because of the lesson from Ninsy and her practice on Ky she understood what she had to do. It wasn't easy though.

Last time she'd fainted, and she couldn't do that again. Not in the middle of a battle. Her own instincts screamed at her not to overdo it, inherently understanding too much would be detrimental to her.

Not that it mattered now. Ky was a beautiful light in this world where she was only a glimmer. It would be worth sacrificing herself for him. The shard at her throat buzzed uncomfortably at that thought.

What had happened between her and Ky today had intertwined their souls. Something inside told her that either of them dying would severely affect the other one.

So, no sacrifice of her life for his, but she would give everything up to that very edge.

Jada spread her arms wide, her naked body feeling the remaining warmth of the day. She and Ky had whiled away every minute of the precious hours in other's arms and bodies.

More time had passed than she realized. The Black Dragon had once again chosen just before dusk for his attack.

That was fine she was comfortable with the dark and her nakedness only added to the sexual component of her magic.

She released the first push of her allure, aiming it toward the Black Dragon. It would also hit Ky, but she hoped that because of their mating, it would not have the same effect on him.

Neither even flinched or seemed to notice.

Okay, she had been too conservative. She opened herself up more and shoved the allure at them.

Both dragons looked over at her. Ky with a beautiful lust in his elongated blue dragon eyes, and Kur-Jara with what she could only describe as irritated surprise.

"Looks like your whore is trying to get my attention."

"She'll get a whole lot more than that from you, piece of dog shit."

The Black Dragon lashed out at Ky with his tail, missing him by mere inches. Ky returned the attack with a blast of ice, encasing the Black Dragon's wings and torso, dropping him to the ground.

Jada loved how she and Ky were working in synchronicity.

The Black Dragon writhed on the ground, and the ice covering half his body melted away. Jada needed to stop screwing around and give it all she had.

She took a deep breath, closed her eyes and thought of Ky's kisses. She gathered the power of the allure into a swirling mass of magic, stepped forward to give this burst all she had, and threw it out into the world.

Every living thing in a one-hundred-yard radius stopped whatever it had been doing and focused on Jada. The birds in the sky, the insects on the ground, the fish in the water, and the dragons in battle.

Both Ky and Kur-Jara dropped to their knees, incapacitated.

Ky lost control of his dragon and shifted back into his human form. Kur-Jara snapped and growled but didn't get up or shift.

"Ky, Are you okay?"

His breathing was heavy, and he didn't respond.

"Looks like you broke your boy toy, succubus whore."

"You really need to find another insult for me besides whore. Work on that, will you?"

The Black Dragon's mouth snapped shut and his head tilted to the side as if he was actually thinking on the problem. Well, good. She was tired of hearing the vitriol coming out of his mouth. Asshole.

Jada ran over to Ky and put her hands on his shoulders. "Look at me."

He obeyed, and when his eyes met hers the lack of anything behind them sent fear crawling through her like snakes on a plane. Horrible and not fun at all.

"Can you hear me?"

Oh Hell, she had broken him. His only response was to stare at her boobs.

"Slut, release me from your bonds."

Seriously? That's his new and improved insult? "Go fuck yourself, you disgusting meat-cicle."

Kur-Jara glared at her as his great claws reached between

his legs and jerked back and forth. Jada gaped at the dragon's literal interpretation of her words.

He was jacking off right there in front of her. It was one of the most bizarre thing she had ever seen.

"You like watching me, slut? Come over here and let me fuck you like a real dragon."

She would need to be careful about what else she said to him. "You don't seem to understand that you are now under my control. So, you can continue to fuck yourself until I say otherwise."

He sneered at her, but she did not fear him anymore. Normally, her allure burned through her as it poured into her victims.

Not today. Not after Ky. She felt as though she could continue to pour the allure out indefinitely, and she still wasn't even using her full capacity. She'd held a small reserve back just in case. Good thing she had because Ky had his own cock in his hands stroking himself with the same instructions as she'd given the Black Dragon.

"Ky Puru, stop. Rest." He kept his eyes on her chest and didn't even as he slumped into the fetal position on the ground.

What the hell was she supposed to do with the two of these dragons now that she had them in her allure? All she done so far was make them touch themselves which when it came to battle strategy seemed pretty damn weak.

Where were the rest of the dragon warriors? Damn, Jakob had told Steele and Dax to escort the women to Fleur's garden. That still left Jakob and Ciara, and she was a white witch with insane powers. Too bad she didn't have any way to contact them. When this was all over, she was getting a phone implanted in her goddamn head. She didn't keep up with technology, but surely that was a thing by now.

Should she risk trying to send Ky back to the house? He did not seem in very good shape right now. Maybe she should try to exile Kur-Jara from their lives while she had him trapped in her allure.

She sure wished they had hashed out more of their plan because she was not good at making decisions.

Never had to.

Ky had put his trust and faith in her. He thought she could do it.

She wouldn't know if she didn't try.

"Tell me why you have sent your demon dragons after me."

Kur-Jara was still stroking himself, and his breathing was heavy. "Because you are a dragon's mate."

That didn't tell her enough. "Why does that matter to you?"

"Fuck you."

She'd asked him a question and hadn't demanded the answer. Kur-Jara's will was strong enough to understand the difference it appeared.

"Tell me why you want the dragons' mates."

Kur-Jara roared, and his semen spilled out onto the ground.

Ew.

The big dragon shook his head and released his cock. It slipped back into his protective scales and he rose up.

"Too late, you whore slut."

He lashed his tail around and smoke poured from his nostrils. He stalked toward her.

Dammit. With his release, the effect of her allure no longer controlled him. His sexual need was slaked. What a dumbass she was.

She opened up that last chunk of her power that she had been holding back. Her instincts screamed at her not to do it. She had no other choice.

The Black Dragon stilled, but she could feel that her hold on him this time was tenuous. She needed to act fast or both she and Ky were dead.

Before she could get her next demand formulated and out of her mouth, Kur-Jara spread his wings, and a mass of demon dragons poured out of the shadows beneath them.

She had no more power to give, and if she tried it would only take away from her hold on Kur-Jara.

Fine. They could take her. Ky would come for her.

The demon dragons raced toward her, and she covered her head with her arms and curled into a ball. The whoosh whoosh whoosh of the demon dragons running past her knocked her over. Not a single one of them even touched her though. She popped her head up to see what the hell was happening.

The demon dragons surrounded Ky and dragged him toward the Black Dragon.

"No. Don't touch him." Her voice was a harsh screech into the air. "Let him go."

The demon dragons completely ignored her, poking and pulling on his limbs. Ky struggled, but was weak. She had no control over them.

"Ky, fight back."

For the first time since she'd landed him with her allure he seemed alert. He thrashed, and his scales shimmered over his body. His talons came out, but he didn't shift.

Had she done that to him?

Ky battled the demon dragons, killing a few before they pinned him to the ground. There were simply too many.

"Your worthless powers are fading. And I grow tired of your bullshit. A Dragon Wyvern is not worth nearly as much as a mate to me, but it will be fun to torture him."

The demon dragons disappeared into the shadow along with Ky.

Blades of fear stabbed her heart. "Stop. Bring him back. Take me instead."

Her words met empty air. The Black Dragon was nothing more than a puff of smoke.

The light from the soul shard around Jada's neck flickered and died. Oh God. Did that mean he was dead?

She wouldn't believe that. They had a deeper connection than that and she was sure she would know if they had killed him.

It would do her no good to search the area for Ky. She knew they had taken him below. Whether he was in the actual underworld or not, he would be in a literal hell.

Jada turned and sprinted across the lawn toward the house. Steel and Fleur owned more land than she'd originally understood. Ky had flown them to the spring in a moment, but it took Jada twenty minutes of running before she even saw the house. Her lungs and muscles screamed at her to stop. Her adrenaline pushed her like a drill sergeant to keep going.

She threw open the front door and yelled out. "Help, anyone here? Help, they've taken him. Please, someone help me." She ran through the house throwing open doors, finding no one.

Where the fuck were Jakob and Ciara?

Had the demon dragons come here too?

She could count on one hand the times in her life she'd

been completely alone. Once when her mother had died and when she'd left the coven a little more than a week ago. The hours before Leon had arrived, she'd been scared, but it was nothing like the fear currently eating her from the inside out, like scarabs in a dead body.

She called upon the one person who had been there for her then and ever since. The one who'd provided her with family and protection, kept her safe from bullshit like this.

If she'd just been content to eat donuts and take the taste of the sex and blood that her coven coveted, Ky wouldn't be...

She couldn't think of what horrors the Black Dragon could be inflicting on him.

Jada smashed a coffee mug someone had left on the table and grabbed a chunk of the broken porcelain. "Bring forth the one who lies upon sleepers, the incubus Leonard, with whom I share the pact of blood and lust."

She used the raw edge of the broken mug, slicing her hand, letting the blood drip to the ground. "Receive this offering. I give it truthfully and willingly."

Smoke rose up from the floor and Leon's form drifted up from the swirls.

"Jada. We have got to get you a fucking phone. Damn it, why are you naked? Isn't that fucking dragon taking care of you?"

Jada ran into Leon's arms, and he slipped off his jacket, covering her before he gave her a hug. "Shh, shh, shh. I'm here."

"They took him. I couldn't stop them. I tried, but I'm not strong enough."

"Oh, tsk, tsk. You're stronger than you think. You just haven't had a chance to spread your wings. Now tell me what happened."

They sat on the nearest couch and Jada told him the main details from the second she met Ky until the Black Dragon disappeared, leaving out the epic sex bits. They wouldn't have bothered Leon, he was an incubus after all, but they were private intimacies between her and Ky.

"That stupid bastard and their god-damned family feud."

The door to the house slammed open and Jakob and Ciara burst through. She was supporting him, and he was covered in blood. Dax was right behind them, then Fleur and a limping Steele.

Jada's friend was missing from the group. "Where's Ninsy?"

Jakob slumped into the nearest chair. "She led the remaining demon dragons on a chase. Told us to retreat here. Where's Ky?"

All Jada could do was shake her head.

Jakob straightened up and scowled. "Where is Ky?"

Leon spoke for her. "Kur-Jara has him."

Jakob, Steele, and Dax were on their feet surrounding her and Leon in an instant. "Who are you?"

Leon had very old power that he could turn on these dragons in an instant if he wanted. "An ally and Jada's father. Her mother entrusted her safety to me until she was claimed. She knew Jada was destined to be a dragon's mate."

A thousand stones could have fallen on Jada in that moment and she wouldn't have felt a thing. Her entire body had gone numb. Her mother had known. No one had ever told her.

Ciara stepped between the warriors and Leon. Jada recognized the soft touch of the white calming power Ciara had wash over her. It had no effect on her, she was too numb.

"Who was this woman and how would she know something like that?"

Leon glanced at Jada and sighed. "I had hoped you would uncover all of this in time yourself. Raina made me swear a binding oath that I wouldn't tell you. She was afraid it would interfere with your destiny."

Jada couldn't look at him. She barely remembered her mother. She'd been gone for hundreds of years, and Jada had been so young when her mother had died. "Who was she? How did she know?"

"Your mother was the daughter of a dragon and the White Witch told her your destiny."

WELCOME TO HELL

*K*y landed hard on the hot stone floor of the barred cave. He was almost grateful for the gravel grinding into the skin on his hands and knees as he pushed himself up. It hurt a hell of a lot less than the whips of fire the demon dragons had lashed him with during the last… he didn't know how long.

What he wouldn't do for an ice lolly.

A scared but tough-girl voice yelled at him. "I'm not telling you shit, asshole, so you can quit skulking over there and get the fuck out."

Skulking?

"Who's there?" Ky used his dragon sight to search for the speaker. It was one of the only parts of his dragon he still had access to.

"Like you don't know. Wait, who the fuck are you?"

Wow, the mouth on this girl. He took a breath, catching her scent. She smelled of the sea, and now that he'd made the connection, he recognized her voice.

"Azynsa?"

She moved into the light at the front of the cave coming from the bubbling lava in the underground hell hole. "Ky Puru?"

She rushed to his side but hesitated to touch him. Probably because there wasn't a whole lot of skin to touch that wasn't burned. "Oh God. What have they done to you?"

"Nothing that won't heal." If he could get access to some water. "What about you? Have they hurt you?"

She shook her head. "Fuckers learned to back the hell off about ten minutes after they dragged me in here from those tunnels where we fought them. They only time I've seen anyone since is when one of the non-imbecilic ones brings me water."

"You don't happen to have any of it now, do you?" His mouth and skin were so dry he felt like he was covered in scales even though he was in his human form.

Thanks to the crone and her scary ass dark magic, he hadn't been able to shift. If he could, he'd find a way to get them both out of there. In his weaker human form, he was a lost cause.

Azynsa slumped and licked her cracked lips. "It's been a while. Couple days I think. Sorry. Can you use your powers to bring some in?"

He was literally in Hell. Azynsa had been dragged in here, so they had to be below the belly of the caldera where she'd been kidnapped.

He opened his senses as far as they could reach, but didn't find the water, an underground spring or even a half-empty bottle of water anywhere.

"It's too hot, and the water is too far away." He'd tried the second his mind had cleared after Jada's allure wore off. He'd blacked out when they sucked him through the shadows. He'd been blissfully wrapped in the magic of Jada's sensuality. The fire whips had been a literal rude awakening.

His mind fought to control the fear for his mate gnawing at his gut. He had no idea if Jada were alive or dead or taken by the Black Dragon. He'd tear Hell down if they were torturing Jada.

It's not like any demons dragons down here wanted to answer his questions about her whereabouts.

He would know if she was dead. Down to his soul, he would know. She must be alive.

"DAMN." Azynsa smacked her dry mouth and slumped into herself. "I was afraid you'd say that. I don't know where we are, but I haven't been able to feel the water since those fuckers dragged down here."

That alone had to be torture for a Mami Wata. But, Ky was grateful they hadn't done worse to her. He'd been afraid that when they'd kidnapped Azynsa she'd be killed. Or worse.

He pulled himself up and rested his side gingerly on the nearest wall. There was no comfortable position, but sitting up was better than lying in the rocks and dirt.

He sure as shit wished he had some shorts. He'd be digging rocks out of his asscrack for weeks after he got out of here.

They would be escaping.

As soon as he could figure out how.

"I told you to bring him to me when you were done with him, crone." A terrible voice, crankier than even Match, roared through the tunnels.

Ah, shit.

The croaking voice of the crone replied, but their words

were growing distant. They must be on the move. "Dispose of him, Kur-Jara. He is mated and of no use to us."

"Shut up. Your revenge lust clouds your insipid brain. Don't interfere…"

Their words faded behind the shuffling and hisses of a pack of demon dragons gathering near the prison cave entrance.

"Azza, get back into the dark. They're coming for me now. They don't need to be reminded you're here."

"No. I can't let them take you." She had a ferocious bravado, he'd give her that. It was a might stronger than his own knowing he was likely in for a hell of a lot more torture at the hands of the Black Dragon.

"We don't have much of a choice. The crone put a spell on me. I can't shift, and I can't heal without the water."

Four demon dragons slithered up to the cave entrance. Two stood guard while the others came in for Ky, and an idea popped into his head.

Azynsa seemed pretty savvy and badass, so hopefully she would go with his spur of the moment plan to get her the fuck out of here.

"Azza. Wait 'til I start fighting back, then make a run for it," he said out of the side of his mouth. "If you get out of here, find any other dragon and get a message to my mate, Jada."

Azynsa's face said no way.

He thought for a moment she was going to refuse, but then she gave him one nod. "What do you want me to say?"

That he was sorry they had such a short time together. "I love her, and I'm fighting."

"Oh Jesus. Okay." She read between the lines. They both knew there was a very real possibility that he wouldn't make it through the next hour, much less get out alive.

But, he would fight. Dragon shift or no. He had the heart of a warrior, not just from his dragon lineage. His Māori ancestors had fought for their way of life more than a century and a half ago. He'd learned to defend himself and strike fear into his enemies before he was old enough to shift.

Back before he'd learned he, or any other dragon warrior, would never have a mate and had built a wall around his heart.

Jada and her beautiful vulnerability, the way she let him in to her heart smashed those defenses.

Yes, he would fight. For her.

The demon dragons rattled the door and slunk closer.

Ky shooed Azynsa. "Now, get back against the wall, but be ready to bolt. I'll keep them occupied as long as I can."

He slumped to the side and put all his weight into his center of gravity. If they wanted to pull him out of here, he wasn't going to be helpful.

"Up. AllFather kill you."

"Great. Ta, but no."

They grunted and growled but backed away. One of them snapped its teeth and pointed at him like that would change his mind. "Up. Up."

They were afraid of him. Even after the beating and the crone's spell, they were fucking terrified that he wasn't simply giving in to their demands.

Best news he'd gotten all day. New plan. He'd scare the shit out of these bastards and injure them the best he could. He and Azynsa were getting the hell out of hell.

Ky groaned as he got to his feet, partially because it really did fucking hurt, and mostly so they would think he was weak and not a threat to them, let down their guard.

He limped his way to the front of the cave and at the last second turned and winked at Azynsa.

His dragon form might not be available to him at the moment, but he knew exactly how to strike fear into the heart of any being, man or beast.

The haka.

But he chose no ordinary rugby haka. If he was going to make it through this day and get back to Jada, he needed some serious inspiration. He'd do the *Tika Tonu* haka.

The ancient dance and chant would be meaningless to the demon dragons, but no matter the words, the haka messed with opponents' heads, whether they were warriors, rugby teams, or demon dragons.

To Ky, the words would invoke Jada for him. *Tika Tonu* was often performed at weddings. He hoped someday to enact this particular haka at his own joining with Jada.

As soon as he was outside of the bars, Ky took up a fighter's stance, legs wide and in a half squat.

"*Ki aro

Kia whakaronga, kia mau!*"

He'd have to chant both the leader's words and the responses. He slapped his thighs and puffed out his chest at the demon dragons. As a group they took one giant step away.

"*Hi!

Ringaringa e torōna

kei waho hoki mai!

Kss Kss.*"

They backed up, looking at each other confused and a little fearful. If they had even a smidgen of intelligence, they'd be thinking he'd gone batshit crazy.

What he was, was crazy in love. The words to his haka

were about becoming a man. Ky would survive this day, and the next. He would be the man Jada needed.

He continued chanting, shouting the words, instilling the passion of every Māori warrior he'd known since birth, his own father, and even Nana Kiki. She'd kick these demon dragons to the dogs and back.

What is right is right. Indeed.

"Tika tonu!

U - e!

Tika tonu!

U... e!"

He waved his arms, raising and dropping his knees, advancing on his enemy and backing them away from Azynsa's escape route.

"Tika tonu atu ki a koe, e tama

Hiki nei koe aku whakaaro, pakia!"

He saw her approach out of the corner of his eye and turned the energy of his dancing and chanting up a notch.

"He hiki aha to hiki?

He hiki roa to hiki?

I a ha hā!"

Azynsa was almost away, but in another meter, she'd be directly in their view. Ky showed the demon dragons his *pukana*, glaring wild-eyed looks. They backed away smelling of urine and fear.

"E tama, te uaua ana

E tama, te mārō

Roa ina hoki ra

Te tohe o te uaua na"

Ky slapped his chest and elbows and prepared to shove the demon boy-band in front of him into each other and then turn and run.

"E tāu nei.

Āna! Āna! Āna! Aue... Hī!"

He growled at the scaredy cats who cowered, and he bolted after Azynsa.

She climbed over rocks and took twisting turns through tunnels. "What the hell was that thing you did? A spell?"

"No, it's a traditional chant about being true to oneself." Oceans, he hoped she knew where she was going. "A dance that will be performed at my wedding."

"Your mate must be one fierce queen."

She was.

Another turn and he could see light. It couldn't be daylight, they were too far underground.

He grabbed at Azynsa's arm, but she practically flew into the open chamber and narrowly avoided running into the Black Dragon by diving behind a pile of rocks.

A dozen demon dragons, given mettle by the mere presence of their king and AllFather, were on him in a second. Ky bellowed and fought. He took one of them out with a well-timed head butt.

Poof.

Splat.

Crack.

He eliminated three more, but there were too many. They pushed him toward the wall and secured his arms and ankles to the rock with scorching metal chains.

"Well, what do we have here? Trying to escape my little corner of hell?"

Ky had been lashed with a fiery whip when the demon dragons first dragged him down. He'd have scars for a long time. But the weapon they'd used on him looked like a kitten's toy ribbon compared to the fire whip in the Black Dragon's hand.

Kur-Jara hadn't yet noticed Azynsa, so Ky went back to plan A. Distract the enemy while she escaped.

The Black Dragon sauntered over and got right up in Ky's face.

Ky pissed on him.

It wasn't much, as dehydrated as he was from being in this heat, but it was definitely enough to *piss* this asshole off.

He shifted into human form, holding his very big, very hot fire whip. "You'll pay for that, you blue piece of shit."

The Black Dragon raised his arm over his head, fire whip poised to lash Ky right down the middle, probably aimed at his junk.

Fuck.

Azynsa popped up from the rocks, rushed between Ky and the Black Dragon and raised her arm, prepared to take the blow from the fire whip.

"No," Ky grunted out.

"Oh yes." Kur-Jara took a few steps back and raised his head in one of those horrible clichéd bad guy laughs. "This is perfect. The unmated mate needs a lesson that will teach her to appreciate just what her life is worth."

He snapped the whip over his head, his muscles bunching, prepared to strike Azynsa. She wouldn't survive the blow.

"Stop." A human woman's voice rang through the cavern. "You will give no lashes to that girl."

Kur-Jara halted, the fire whip poised over his shoulder. He narrowed his eyes and turned to find the speaker. His body hid her from Ky and Azynsa's view. "Tell me why not. I am lashing someone today, damn it."

He was different with this woman than he had been with the crone. He didn't call her names like a school-boy.

The woman, walked across the room and stood in front of the two of them. With her raven-black hair and lilly white skin, she looked a lot like Jada. There was no way she could be human and survive down here. Maybe she was a demon too. Ky didn't scent that on her. Maybe his senses were all out of whack without his dragon.

She closed her fists and glanced back at Ky and Azynsa. Fire lit up her eyes. Literal fire. Flames burned where her pupils should be.

If she was human, they had done some fucked up shit to her down here to make that happen.

"Why shouldn't I give her the lashes she has coming, Fallyn? She's proven worthless to me without the shard. She's nothing more than a dragon's whore."

"It. Is. Not. Her. Birthday."

"Ah. But it is yours. I had almost forgotten." Kur-Jara paced. "Take her lashes and yours and I will let the mate go. For now."

"I will take her lashes, but in exchange neither you nor my brothers will touch her. The punishment today will serve for her upcoming birthday, whenever it may be."

Every sentence that came out of her mouth raised more and more questions. Birthday? Her brothers?

"Very well, little red devil."

This woman certainly wielded more control than the crone. Just who the hell was she?

His mate?

No. It couldn't be.

Jada had said the demon dragons were Kur-Jara's

offspring. If that's who she was referring to when she said brothers, this family was all kinds of fucked up.

"Come, little daughter. Lay across that rock there so that the dragon and the whore can watch your tears, and so that I can see their pain in your pain."

The woman, Fallyn, took the position, laying on her stomach across the rock, gripping chains that had been drilled into it.

Ky jerked against the restraints holding him against the wall. He could not let this woman get whipped. Daughter of the king of hell or not, she didn't deserve this.

She stared at him for a moment and then gave one sharp shake of her head, before she lowered her eyes staring at nothing.

"How old are you, whore?" the Black Dragon rumbled.

Fallyn didn't respond.

"Fishy bitch. I asked how old you are. Don't make me guess, because I assure you I will over estimate."

"Why does that matter?" The fight and vigor had gone out of Azynsa's voice, her words filled with a tremor.

"Because Fallyn is taking your lashes. One for each year old you are."

Azynsa shook her head and clamped her hands over her mouth.

"Tell me now or I'll just make it an even hundred."

"No," she cried out. "I'm not that old. That's not fair."

Kur-Jara blew a stream of fire over the whip, boosting its flames. "One hun—"

"Twenty-three," she blurted. "I'm only twenty-three."

"Fine."

Fuck. He was going to lash Fallyn twenty-three times. Ky couldn't allow it.

The whip cracked through the air smacking the woman's back, slicing open her thick leather tunic. She didn't even flinch.

"One," she said.

Two more and her shirt fell away all together. Still she counted and barely moved as the fire bit her skin.

Ky's dragon roared, fighting to come out, scratching and clawing to get to the surface. The crone's spell held fast.

"Four, five, six." Her body took the strikes, but the pain came through in the way she counted through gritted teeth.

Ky jerked at the chains using all of his strength to try and pry them free. Even if he couldn't shift, he could put his body between that whip and the girl sacrificing herself.

Jada would kill him, when she finally met him in the afterlife.

"Seven, eight, nine, ten." Her voice wavered on the last number, affected by the pain of the lashes.

Ky's scales skittered across his skin. The tattoo on his arm and shoulder writhed, trying to get him moving.

When the count hit twenty, Azynsa turned away, her hands over her mouth, so much pain written across her face.

Ky could handle his own pain. But seeing this woman, a human he should be protecting, one who reminded him of Jada, suffer even though she tried her best not to show it, shredded him.

What if this bastard had captured Jada?

He'd made his own wrists raw fighting the shackles. They'd be bloody if he wasn't so damn dry.

Ky's heart literally hurt at the thought of Jada in this monster's hold. He had to get out of here and make sure those fucking demon dragons never got anywhere near her.

"How could I have done that to her?" Azynsa whispered.

Her face was streaked with two tear tracks she'd tried her best to hide.

"Don't turn your hatred inward, sister. Focus it all on the beast. It will help us when we find a way to kill him and get out of here."

Azynsa gulped in an escaped sob. "It's my fault. If I hadn't tried to stop him, to stand up to him, this wouldn't have happened. I never fucking learn."

She sniffed and wiped at her cheeks, smearing the tear tracks with the ash in the air.

Tears.

Water.

"Azza. Got any more of those tears left in you, sweetheart? Bring them on over here. You may have just given us our first break."

"I don't know. I'm surprised I cried as much as I did. I'm so damn dehydrated."

"Try for me, will you?"

The Black Dragon meted out the final three lashes. Not once did Fallyn cry out, but the pain was written in her bunched muscles, the lines in her face. She was one tough cookie.

Thank the First Dragon that was over.

Those last three snaps of the fire whip pushed another tear from Azynsa's eyes and Ky concentrated on the little droplet and the remaining wetness on her face. He didn't need much, but it was hotter than Hades down here and dryer than the Akashic plane. The moisture in that one tear wouldn't last long.

He pulled it to him and spun it around and around like a water saw, grinding away at one link in the shackles that bound him. He only needed it to erode away enough of the metal to weaken the link.

A thin line bored into the metal, but the drop evaporated within a few revolutions. Shit.

If he had even an ounce of spit, he'd use it. But, every organ in his body was shriveling up by the second from lack of water.

"Azza?"

She shook her head and slumped to the floor at his feet. "I…don't have anything left. I'm sorry."

Kur-Jara chuckled, having enjoyed his activity. Would he keep his word and leave Azynsa alone?

"There, cowardly bitch. She's taken your lashes."

Azynsa slowly turned to look at Fallyn. She mouthed the words "I'm sorry," but Ky didn't think Fallyn saw.

"Tell the nice people how old you are today, daughter. How many lashes you'll get for your birthday."

Fallyn raised her head and wrapped the chains from the rock around her hands in another turn.

"One-hundred and fifty-six."

Azynsa gasped and the tears she did not think she had flowed down the dirty tracks on her face.

"One."

RETREAT, HELL

The dragons wanted to mount a rescue but didn't know where to start. Leon knew more about the king of hell, the Black Dragon, than any of them.

So, Jada let them hash out the details and stepped back from any sort of participation in the plan. They had listened to her before and look what happened.

Ky had believed in her, and now he was in hell. Literally.

She hadn't had to make a decision since she was five and which dessert she wanted was still the extent of what kind of choices she should be allowed to make.

Leon suggested they retreat to the Cape where his coven could defend against the demon dragons, should they attack before a rescue attempt could be made.

Jada tried to talk the dragons and their mates out of coming to Leon's house. Demons and dragons just didn't mix all that often, and it was probably going to be a weird reunion with her return anyway.

She couldn't face the judgment she would receive from her

brothers and sisters of the coven for leaving in the first place, especially Portia. If she was still alive.

Jada swallowed past the tightness in her throat. Portia had always been her only ally. They'd bonded over being the only half-human's in the coven. But Portia was always stronger than she was, never took guff from the others.

As screwed up as they were, the coven was her family. Even if they had kept too many secrets from her.

Especially Leon.

He'd kept the biggest secret of all.

The house on the Cape felt even colder to her than before she'd left, like a girl running away from home. Maybe because her short time with Ninsy and then the dragons had so much life.

The dozen other incubi and succubae were milling around one half of the great room, and the dragons and their mates were huddled on the other side. She didn't see Portia though.

Leon strode to the middle of the room and clapped his hands to get everyone's attention. His story about her mother, the White Witch, and her destiny to be a dragon's mate had her stomach feeling like it was in the highest speed of her six hundred-dollar KitchenAid stand mixer.

She stood off to the side, trying to hide and waiting for anyone to tell her what to do. Ciara approached her, and Jada had a hard time looking her in the eye. This was a powerful woman who had done what she needed to when her mate had been in danger. What must she think of Jada and her failure?

"How are you holding up, Jada?" Ciara slid her hand up and down Jada's arm, trying to comfort. Not even Ciara's talent with emotions could change how Jada felt inside. Because she felt nothing. It was like a big empty expanse where her feelings used to be.

"I'm fine."

"Yeah, no. That's code for super shitty if ever I've heard it. But I get it. This whole being a dragon's mate thing isn't all kisses and daisies."

That was strange coming from someone who seemed so damn happy and in love with her man.

"You're looking at me like I sprouted a rhinoceros horn." Ciara patted her forehead. "Nope, I guess that means you're just surprised to hear me say that."

Jada nodded. "Uh, yeah. You two seem tight."

"We are. But that has taken some time. They lead dangerous lives and it's getting worse all the time. That fear and worry that they might survive a battle, that they won't come home…it's really hard to live with. A lot of my attitude about becoming a Dragon's mate changed when Jakob died."

Holy guacamole. "What?"

"Not that long ago, in the last big battle against the demon dragons, Jakob was trying to protect me and –" Ciara swallowed hard. "He… died. Right there in front of me, practically in my arms."

Jada looked over to where Jakob was talking with the others, then back at Ciara. Jakob looked pretty alive to her. "So, what happened?"

"This is going to sound super corny, but I think it was love. Love conquered all." Ciara laughed. "I warned you it would sound corny."

"Your love for him brought him back from the dead?" Jada would apologize to Ciara later for sounding so incredulous, even if she'd gotten the corny warning.

"I think so. He gave me his soul right before he died and it meant so incredibly much to me that all of my emotions and powers went wackadoodle. Then, poof, he was back."

"You mean he gave you his soul shard." Nothing like that had happened to her when Ky gave his talisman over to her.

"No, I mean yes, he did give me the shard. But that's not what I meant. He gave me his soul. Actually, said it was already mine. All I did was accept it."

Jada was the one who had a hard time swallowing now. Ky had said something similar to her before they had been attacked.

Was he gone now because she hadn't truly accepted the gift he was giving her?

She would have to think about it later, or maybe never, because a commotion started on the other side of the room. Her brothers and sisters were murmuring and getting louder by the second. Then the crowd split, and Portia was shoved from the center of the group and skidded onto the floor.

Leon raised his hands into the air and waited for everyone to quiet. When they did he addressed Portia. "You have been punished once before for disobeying the laws of this coven."

Oh no, was Leon really going to do this in front of all the dragons? It wasn't like him air family business in front of others.

Whatever he was going to do now, must have something to do with why he insisted they all retreat back here. Leon had brought the dragons here to his home for a reason. He knew something important that the dragons would care about.

Jada was not making the connection between Portia and the dragons though.

"If it were up to me," Leon continued, "I would ban you for life, and we both know that's a very long time. But I'm not the one you wronged. I won't be meting out your punishment."

Portia glanced between Jada and Leon and shook her head in fear. "No, ban me. I'll leave."

"That's not how this works. Now tell your sister your offense against her."

Jada glanced at all the other women in the coven trying to figure out who Portia had harmed. None of them cared for her, but it had never bothered Portia. It had always been harder for Jada not to care.

"She has the heart of the human, so maybe she'll go easy on you," Leon said and waved his arm indicating Jada.

Me? Portia had helped her, not harmed her.

Portia looked up at Jada, sorrow and pain written in all her features. No, Jada wouldn't believe it. What could Portia have done to her that would make her feel this bad?

"Tell her, Portia. Or I will."

Tears fell from Portia's eyes and the rest of the coven recoiled. They had a disdain for emotional outbursts from their half human sisters. She and Portia had both learned not to cry in front of them. Portia shook her head and then looked at the floor.

Leon grabbed Portia by the arm and lifted her to her feet. "Your sister here told Kur-Jara where to find you and your mate."

Jada had never felt the burn of betrayal. It hurt so much more than if any other member of the coven had done this to her. They'd relied on each other, been there when no one else would be. This couldn't be happening. "Portia?"

Portia wouldn't look at her and that alone told Jada that it was the truth. "Why? I don't understand. Why would you do this to me, to us?"

Portia had been her friend, the closest thing she had to a true sister. She thought they understood each other.

Leon shook Portia's arm until she tore it away. "Because,

Jada," her voice was shaky and pleading. "You are not the only mate of a Dragon."

Portia tore her shirt open to reveal a golden shard on a cord, identical to the ones that Ciara and Fleur wore. Jada had no doubt in her mind what it was. Cage Gylden's soul shard.

It didn't have the light inside like the bone carving that contained Ky's soul shard around Jada's neck. It lay against Portia's skin cold and dead.

The dragons rushed toward Portia. "You're the succubus that stole Cage's shard. He's dying because of you."

Jada held up her hand and stopped the dragons from advancing on Portia. "What's going on?"

Portia pressed her lips together and didn't say another word.

Leon rolled his eyes and shook his head. "She exchanged your mate for hers."

Portia slumped, her final secret revealed. "Geshtianna is holding him hostage. It's why I got in trouble the last time. I knew Leon would send me to her for my ban. She told me if I could get a dragon soul shard she would let my mate go."

Jakob growled low, and Jada didn't blame him. "Then why do you still have it? Why aren't flitting off into the sunset with this dragon of yours, if there even is one?"

"She wouldn't release him. She said the shard itself wasn't enough. And if I wanted her to let Jett go, she needed more. I had to get her the location of another dragon's mate. One that hadn't yet been given a soul shard." Portia glanced around at everyone else in the room, her eyes hovering over Ciara and Fleur. "Do you know how many dragons' mates there are? None. There were those two or nothing. Until you. When I saw you with that dragon, I knew right away. I'm sorry."

Jada walked up to her sister. Even that word hurt her now.

She looked Portia straight in the eye and slapped her across the face.

The coven, Portia, they weren't her family. Ky was.

Jada didn't wait to listen to Portia's pleas. She walked away and waited until she was out of the room and could hide behind closed doors before she broke into tears.

Leon was the first to find her a few minutes later in the mansion's kitchen. It was almost a relief. She didn't think she could face Ciara, Fleur, or any of the dragons.

It wasn't like the kitchen was the best hiding place. No one else in the coven ever used it. She'd only been gone a little more than a week, but with mostly full-blooded demons there weren't a lot of ingredients to make anything.

Half the stuff in the refrigerator had spoiled and no one had noticed. She threw most of it in the trash but did find a stray stick of butter she hadn't used in her last recipe. There was also still flour, eggs, sugar, and—best of all—milk chocolate chips. She had every intention of putting a batch in the oven to share with the dragons and their mates, but here she sat eating cookie dough straight out of the bowl.

"You can't hide from this one behind cookies," Leon said.

"It's not cookies, it's cookie dough." Leon had never understood her need for comfort food. Mostly because the kind of food that comforted him came from a vein. But warm delicious smells from the kitchen was one of the only memories she still had of her mother. She'd made cookies just like this, and breads, and pies, which was probably why Jada had been a chubby child.

She knew that she retreated to the warm scents of the kitchen because those few short years before her mother had died had been… peaceful.

Everything since, not so much.

There was only one other person Jada felt a connection with like that.

Portia had always been the only other one who got it. They'd shared many things growing up, including mealtime. Nobody else relished a cheeseburger like Portia did.

Now, they shared something else in common.

"She's much better suited to be a dragon's mate than I am. Look how she put everything on the line for her mate. I barely even know Ky, and I've been too wrapped up in my own baloney to try to have feelings for him."

"You two always were like peas in a pod. Both trying to push that human side of you away. Dumb bunnies."

"What were we supposed to do? We're half demon, we grew up in and live in a house full of demons, our father is a demon, and you're the one always pushing sex and blood on us."

Leon sighed and scrubbed his face as if he were tired. Leon didn't get tired. "It's not like I raised a half human child destined to be the mate of a dragon before, is it?"

Well crap. She hadn't meant to make him feel bad. What did Leon know about love? Sex, yeah. But real love, like what she had squirreled away in her heart for Ky, Leon would understand it even less than heated chocolate chip cookies.

"Your mom probably wouldn't have approved of the way I raised you either. I'm not sure sometimes she hasn't come back to haunt me. But I did my best to keep you safe all these years, waiting on that stupid dragon to come find you."

Was that a hint of regret in Leon's voice? Another feeling he didn't ever have.

"Why did you seduce my mother?" And more importantly, why hadn't she died like most other incubus victims? Leon had the ability to control his blood lust because he didn't have those same emotions, so he could let his victims live if he wanted to. But it was rare that he did.

It was a lot easier to dispose of a body than avoid an investigation.

"Oh, ho, ho. I'm pretty sure your mother was the one doing the seducing."

That was interesting. Jada kept her mouth shut, hoping Leon would just tell the story.

"That woman had a natural allure. It was magical, pure sensuality. She had those lush hips and—"

"Whoa. Stop right there. I know you well enough to understand where this is going. I do not want to hear about your sex life with my mother."

Leon chuckled and stuck his finger into the cookie dough. He frowned at it, poking at the dough a few more times testing its consistency. Then he pulled his finger out, sniffed, and licked it. He made that not–bad face. "Hmm."

This day was turning out to be even weirder than she thought it already was.

"Anyway, I almost gave it all up for her."

Really fucking weird. Give all what up? Jada opened and closed her mouth several times, not sure what words to say.

"Yeah, you're not the only one who looked at me that way when I decided to stay with her. In the end, she was the one who talked me out of it."

Leon stuck his finger in the cookie dough again and tried a chocolate chip this time. He made a face at her and spit it out. After he wiped his mouth, he said something Jada was sure would stick with her for the rest of her life.

"I'm going to tell you the same thing Raina told me." He clapped both hands on Jada's shoulders and smiled down at her. Leon didn't smile that often. "You have to be who you were meant to be. I'm not talking about what destiny says or fate. But who you know you are inside. We all wear a façade of what we think the world wants to see from us, but the more you hide what you truly are, the more miserable you will be. I won't hold you back, because you'll be miserable if you stay. I know you think this is what you want, and it might be for a little while. But your heart lies elsewhere. We both know that. You have to go. I'll always be here, we'll always be here."

A sensation like Jada had never felt before settled in her chest. It was like when the sun went down over the ocean and threw a million sparkles out over the water. Like the smell of fresh baked apple pie. Like curling up with a kitten on your lap and a book you've been longing to read.

Jada let go of the breath she hadn't realized she was holding. She'd fought against the pull of her heart toward Ky from the get-go. Even when he had been gentle and soft with her, she didn't know how to act, how to be. She had continually second-guessed her every move, every look, every word. None of it had ever felt right, but not because of Ky, because of her.

A tiny fraction of her debilitating self-doubt washed away in Leon's story, his advice. Her mother's advice.

It wasn't all gone by any means. But Leon and Ky had pried open a door for her to step through on the path toward being and accepting herself.

Leon smiled sadly. "I didn't understand until years later that when she said we'll always be here, she meant her and you. I left before you were even born and didn't return until she summoned me."

Jada knew the rest of that story. Her mother had gotten cancer and died on a Tuesday.

"So, tell me, fruit of my loins, who do you want to be?"

Jada wasn't a hundred percent sure, but she knew she wasn't going to hide anymore.

She wouldn't hide in the coven, she wouldn't hide from the demon dragons, and she wouldn't hide from the one thing in her life that she'd ever truly wanted. Love.

"I don't know. But let's start with I want to be the person who rescues my dragon in distress."

ROUGH NIGHT

Fallyn's sacrifice did not save Ky from receiving his own lashes. Instead of using Azynsa's tears to work himself free of the chains he called upon the inherent power in the element to encase his dwindling life force.

He knew it would cut him off from Jada, and since he had given her his soul, she would be freaking out that she couldn't feel him.

But, this was pure survival mode. He had hoped that Fallyn had secured Azynsa's release. But as soon her birthday punishment had ended, she left and didn't take Azynsa with her.

Ky couldn't blame her. He'd had a fourth as many lashes as that woman and was on the verge of death. He didn't understand how she had survived.

He didn't understand how he had survived.

Azynsa had thrown a fit and protested each strike of Kur-Jara's whip, until demon dragons dragged her away, presumably back to the cell. She would be okay for now. He couldn't

say as much for the demon dragons who hauled her off. One
or two of them were probably missing their balls by now.

The cavern was dark except for a muted glow from the
nearby lava pit. He wasn't sure if it was because the crone had
used her magic to dampen the light or if his own vision was
fading. Probably the latter, since he hadn't seen the crone
after her dressing down by the Black Dragon.

Ky still hung on the wall, not having been freed when Kur-
Jara was finished with him. They might've all thought he was
actually dead.

He kind of felt like he was, drifting in and out of
consciousness ,and his head felt stuffed with wool.

This was exactly what he thought the afterlife would look
like, all hazy and filled with dragons and beautiful women.

Uhh...

"What the hell is up with these dumbass dragons?"

Uh-oh. Either he was hallucinating, or he had really died.
Because a dazzling woman in white and a very cranky-faced
but colorful dragon appeared before him.

"I don't think this one is dumb, dear. He did what he was
supposed to– mark, claim, mate, and in record time I might
add. But his mate is a little tougher than the others."

Were they talking about him and Jada? She wasn't tough.
Don't get him wrong, she was a badass, but she also had a soft
vulnerable heart.

He tried to open his mouth to say that but couldn't.

"Don't try to speak, Kaiārahi Tarakona Puru. You need to
save your energy. That little spark of life that you protected
with your element is fighting to keep you alive. Good thing
you already gave your soul to Jada."

The woman approached him and pressed her hand against
his chest. A soft blue light warmed him from the inside, but

also felt like a cool balm to his injuries. His dragon stretched and basked in the glow.

"We can't stay long, son. Were only here to give you a little advice." The big dragon's voice had a similar power to it as when Ky used his alpha voice to hand out commands to his Wyr.

Match had a similar voice when he needed to use his alpha of alphas status. But this Dragon had so much more. Could he possibly be?

The dragon grinned or showed his teeth in a grin-like grimace and nodded. *"I know what you're thinking, my boy, and the answer is yes."*

Holy First Dragon. It was the First Goddamn Dragon. So that meant… she was the White Witch.

Shit. He was dead.

No. He couldn't be dead. He'd just found Jada. The witch had said his water element had protected him and that Jada still had his soul.

But, if he wasn't dead, how the hell was he hearing the First Dragon talk to him?

"Yes, I have always been this handsome. See that scale right there," he said and used a talon to point to one particular scale on his chest with a brilliant blue color, *"that's where you get your color from."*

"Sweetheart. There are a lot of Galla dragons around. I don't think we have time for your preening."

The First Dragon leaned forward and not so quietly whispered, *"She loves my preening, especially when it comes to my cock. I manscape for her, you know. You should think about doing that too."*

TMI, First Dragon, TMI.

Also, manscaping? The First Dragon was thousands of

years old when he'd died, over seven hundred years ago. How did he know about manscaping?

Shouldn't it be called dragonscaping?

Ky's head was going to explode.

He did not need to know about the first Dragon and the White Witch's sex life. Oceans, he hoped they didn't know about his. If they were some sort of spirits from the afterlife, they could probably go around spying on any of their children, checking in to see if they are being naughty or nice.

Ky had definitely been naughty—very, very naughty—when it came to sex with Jada. He had every intention of getting naughtier. Assuming these two were here to help him get out of here and back to her.

He wondered if anyone else had ever imagined the first Dragon wearing a Santa hat. The White Witch could totally pull off a sexy Mrs. Claus costume.

Holy brain melt, what was he saying?

"I don't think preening means what you think it means." The First Dragon rolled his eyes for only Ky to see. Then he whispered again this time so that the White Witch wouldn't hear. *"She thinks I'm as dumb as you."*

She smacked him on the wing. "He's not dumb. Kur-Jara is getting more aggressive. We didn't expect him to go this far, at least not this soon."

Wait, so that meant that the First Dragon and the White Witch new about Kur-Jara's evil plans.

They needed to tell him. Ky tried to get their attention but got out nothing more than a small groan.

The White Witch turned her back on him, and Ky swore he saw her put her hand to her mouth, as if she were holding back sobs. Before he could even be sure though, she moved away. "You two talk a little shop, I'm going to try to find our little red dragon."

If there was another dragon down here, they should try to escape together. There was no way they were talking about Match, were they? If his brother Wyverns had mounted a rescue mission, they could mean Match.

"Damn. I upset her." The First Dragon paced in front of Ky, clearly not thinking about the advice he was supposed to be giving. Ky was in no position to remind him.

"You'd think after a couple of centuries, I'd have her figured out. Women. Am I right? You've got your hands full with that pretty little succubus."

Ky would gladly have his hands full of Jada. He adored the way her ass filled his hands, her tits filled his mouth, Jada's heart filled his soul.

"Well, I've pissed her off already. Might as well go big or go home."

The First Dragon raised his head and stared down at Ky with an intensity that bore into him.

"Because she's not here, and can't hear us, I will let you in on a little secret, boy. But if you tell her I said anything, I'll turn your scales brown with orange polka dots. You got me? "

It wasn't like Ky was going to refuse.

"There're a lot of mates running around these parts. You get that mermaid girl and get her out of here. Your brother's been waiting on her."

So Azynsa was a mate. But whose? By brother did he mean a dragon or one of the other Wyverns? If a mermaid was going to be anyone's mate, she'd be best suited to a blue. Ky couldn't imagine her with a gold. Where would they live?

He felt like he should say yes, sir. But he still hadn't recovered his voice.

"And you boys watch out for the Black Dragon's youngling."

Which one? There were like a million demon dragons, not to mention the Black Dragon's daughter.

"That kid is both friend and foe. I wish we had figured out a way to get him out and raised right. He'll be just as powerful as his father someday. It will depend on you all and his mate which way it goes."

In his wildest imagination, he'd never considered that one of the demon dragons had the smarts to be anything but a tool. Not a leader, certainly not a friend, but they were all pretty horrible foes.

No fucking way any demon dragon deserved a mate.

The First Dragon smacked Ky on the head with a tap of his tail. His brain went off like a 3D movie with the memory of Ciara's story about a man in the forest outside of Jakob's villa when she had escaped. She had sworn there had been a demon dragon fighting off more of the bastards. Then again, she had said this mystery demon dragon was in her apartment during their battle and had relinquished Jakob's soul to her.

Ky hadn't been able to identify this demon dragon's scent, and the other Wyverns couldn't account for him either. The Wyverns had decided he was some sort of a rogue. He had to be the youngling the First Dragon was warning him about. Being the son of a Black Dragon certainly made him someone to watch out for.

The White Witch popped back into the room and slid underneath the First Dragon's wing. She snuggled into him and closed her eyes.

Ky hadn't thought a supernatural being like the White Witch would need comforting.

The two rested together like that for only a heartbeat before the White Witch recovered and patted the First Dragon's scales.

"We must go. Any longer and my sister will feel our presence. She's going to be pissed I ruined her spell. Like she isn't already mad and out for revenge."

Ky wasn't ready for them to leave. He still didn't know the Black Dragon's plans, and he wasn't completely healed. How was he supposed to get himself and Azynsa out of here?

If only he had a little water.

The White Witch came up to Ky and kissed him on the forehead. "You take care of your mate, Ky. She still thinks she has to hide her true self away for you to love her. Prove her wrong."

"Yeah, and then for good measure give her a good couple dozen orgasm. Mates like that."

Ky's brain fizzled, first from the sex advice from the First Dragon, but then in a nice way, like going back to bed on a Sunday morning.

Ky blacked out, and when he blinked open his eyes, the room filled with the glowing light from the lava again, but no First Dragon or White Witch.

At least she had healed him quite a lot. The burns on his body weren't even tender anymore. He looked down, and only a few scars remained. Sweet as.

Ky hadn't exactly had favor on his side today, but it appeared he had the First Dragon and the White Witch on his team.

He yanked at the chains, damn tired of waiting to be rescued.

So far, Match sucked at this game. He should have been here by now if they were in fact in the bottom of the caldera in Africa.

Ky growled out his frustration and jerked as hard as he could against the chains. They popped out easily, as if he had had the strength of his dragon, and he tumbled to the floor.

In front of him, digging into the porous lava rock, were talons, blue ones.

His talons. He dragged his gaze along his forearms and saw scales instead of skin.

He took a deep breath and blew out a frigid puff of air.

Fuck yeah.

He had his dragon back.

He used his dragon sight to peer into the dark tunnels and try to find both his enemies and his little mermaid. He didn't see Azynsa anywhere, but the Black Dragon, followed by a shit ton of demon dragons, was headed his way.

"You stupid shits. How fucking hard is it to find one half human woman when I tell you exactly where the fuck she is." Ooh, the dickhead was mad. Poor baby.

That filled Ky with a little bit of joy. Jada was safe for a little longer.

"You made them too stupid, you old hag."

"They're from your genes, not mine. My suppression spells only do so much." The crone shot back. Even she wasn't taking shit from the Black Dragon.

Strange. Why would Kur-Jara have the crone suppress anything in his offspring? When Ky got out of here, and it was when now, not if, he had a lot of intel to bring back to the AllWyr. Then Jakob and Match could hash out what all these questions meant. Ky was taking a fucking vacation. Just him and Jada in a secluded little cove, where they could have plenty of sex on the beach, and not the drinks.

The ruckas of the arguing baddies was close now. This was Ky's chance to kick the Black Dragon's ass. He hadn't had a chance to stretch the increase in powers he'd felt when he and

Jada mated. It had been curtailed by her powerful allure. But, now that he knew what that felt like, the next time she used her powers he would be ready to harness it and add hers to his own.

But the First Dragon had given him the mission to get Azynsa out of here.

On one claw, the odds were stacked against him in a battle. This was their home turf and there were a lot more of them. He had no doubt he could take a lot of the demon dragons out, and at least injure the Black Dragon. He wasn't sure he'd make it out of that battle with enough energy to find Azynsa and escape.

Damn, he hated leaving this opportunity untaken.

He would go find Azynsa and he would get back to Jada as soon as he could. In one more minute. Anything else he could glean from eavesdropping on the enemy would help them win the war. Loose lips sink shits. Lots and lots of demon dragon shits.

Their voices were getting louder, and he would only have a few moments. Now that he was back and in dragon form, it wasn't like he could hide behind a rock.

He had a plan that involved grabbing Azynsa and stretching his senses to find the tunnels leading to the tide pool. Come hell or hopefully high water, they'd get out of here quickly.

"Yes, I know the succubus went back to her coven. Stupid bitch. Leonard can only protect her for so long."

Ky had missed something. Why had Jada gone back to Leon?

"The dragons have forsaken her for taking the golden shard. She won't be safe for long," the crone said, gleefully.

If Ky's heart had plummeted any further it would have

fallen right out of his chest, rolled across the floor, and into the lava. Jada had taken Cage's soul shard.

No. He wouldn't believe it. He would've known. She trusted him; she would've told him.

"She still thinks she has to hide her true self for you to love her." That's what the White Witch had said. "She's tougher than the others."

Now Ky understood what that meant.

Being Jada's mate would be tough on him if she couldn't be trusted.

His soul screamed that couldn't be right. She was his soulmate—his true mate. He loved her. Fate would not have given him a mate he could not trust.

He had no idea if that was true or not. He had no information to go on. The only other dragons who had mates were Jakob and Steele. They were both beyond happy in their relationships.

But before the greens found mates, it had been generations. What if this happened all of the time back then, making enemies lovers? There was no one to ask.

Ky was so distracted that he didn't even notice the enemy had found him until there were three demon dragons on his back.

He roared and swatted them away, using the deep hurt and anger at Jada's betrayal to fuel his battle. All three of the demon dragons who attacked him first hit the cavern wall so hard they instantly exploded into ash.

"Get him," Kur-Jara roared. The man shifted into his own big Black Dragon and spewed fire at Ky's head.

Ky jump to the air and dive bombed the Black Dragon, aiming his talons for its eyes.

The Black Dragon shot another spout of flame at Ky, but

he defended with an icy blast. He still had no water, but he could control the temperature of the air, ice being part of his element.

He had enough fury in him to turn half the horde into ice cubes, which he scooped up and threw like some little projectile icicles at the Black Dragon's head.

When he ran out of demon dragons to throw, he could throw the ice formed around his heart. Until he saw Jada again and found out the truth of whether she had betrayed all of Dragonkind, and him, his heart would be guarded like it should have been from the start.

He'd opened himself too early, loved her too fast.

From here on out, his heart would be as hard as stone and cold as ice.

BETRAYAL

*J*ada walked back into a shitstorm brewing between the dragons and the demons. Ciara had her hands raised in the air and snowflakes swirled through the grand hall. Her magic calmed them, but there was still a standoff. Leon had beat her into the room and stood nose to nose with Jakob.

"I don't want to start a war with you too, incubus, but I will if we don't walk out of here with that soul shard." Jakob's words had a whole new ring to them, one that had a lot more power behind it than Jada had ever heard before.

"It's not my call, dragon. You will not interfere with the one who gets to make the choice." Leon was a hell of a lot older than Jakob. Maybe as old as their First Dragon.

Jada did not want to see the Green Dragon Wyvern and Leon throw down. But, she certainly wasn't the one making decisions around here.

"Then, who is?" Ciara asked. Jada sensed Ciara's emotional hold on Jakob was slipping. She put her hand on his arm and his clenched fist dropped open.

"Only the ones Portia has wronged can decide her fate. That is how it works in the coven. Since the dragon whose soul she has stolen is not here, the one she has betrayed will have to decide what to do with her."

Every single eye in the room turned to Jada.

Crap oh rama.

Leon's gaze was the most penetrating. He'd made every decision in her life for her for years. "What do you want to do, Jada? You can do anything from permanently ban her up to death."

Oh no. She couldn't keep her voice from shaking. "Death?"

"Yes." Leon nodded. "She threatened both your life and the life of your mate. It's fair for you to threaten hers in return, even take it."

Jada had heard that other covens were much more brutal than Leon's. But it was only ever rumors. Leon was strict with them, but Portia's last punishment was the first one they'd had in years.

Jada wondered what could have happened to Portia when she had been banned and sent to Geshtianna's coven. That month turned her friend and sister against her. She had a hard time believing that this whole thing was over a guy.

If Portia felt anything like what Jada felt for Ky, she could understand.

If this were truly her decision, she needed to make it count. She wouldn't set the example to the coven or the dragons that her demon side controlled her. She could overcome her darkness. She would live in the light. "I won't harm Portia."

The coven side of the room erupted in protests. Jada raised her hand, and surprisingly they quieted. "I don't deny that her betrayal has cut me deep. I'm not sure it's a wound that can be healed."

Any anger Portia had over her current circumstances slipped from her face and she replaced it with guilt and sadness. They both knew things would never be the same between them, and that hurt almost as badly. Portia swallowed several times and then dropped her eyes.

"I choose instead of punishment, reparation. Portia will return the soul shard she stole, take us to her mate, and then together they will help us rescue mine."

Portia's head shot up and she gasped. "Geshtianna's coven is a dangerous place. She may well kill me for bringing you and the dragons there. Send me in alone. I swear to bring Jett out and help you find your mate."

"I wish that I could trust you. But you know that I can't." That made Jada so sad. Instead, she would have to learn to trust in herself.

Portia nodded.

Leon shooed the other demons away. "Pack what you want to take with you, Portia. While Jada will not ban you as her punishment, I will. If we cannot trust and rely on each other, we cannot be family. Once your mission to help Jada and the dragons recover what you have taken from them is complete, do not return to us."

A heavy lump hung in Jada's throat and tears pricked her eyes. The woman she had grown up with, her only friend, would no longer be a part of her family. She wanted to take it all back and say everything was okay. But it wasn't and they would both be dealing with the fallout for a long time to come.

Portia left the great room and Leon circled the dragons to talk. "Portia is not wrong when she says Geshtianna's coven is dangerous. She's almost as old as I am and has had a grudge against your kind forever, both she and her brother Dumuzid."

Jakob didn't exactly look concerned at that news, but thoughtful. "Do you know why?"

Leon shook his head. "No idea. But demons have long memories. So, whatever it was probably happened a very long time ago, and it's been boiling and bubbling in her ever since. You won't be safe there, even a little bit. Get in and get out as fast as you can."

"You're not coming?" Jada had hoped Leon would help smooth the way with Geshtianna.

"No, she and I have our own age-old feud. Besides, you know I don't really like the desert or the demons who live there. They're all so old and stuffy over there." Leon reached into the pocket of his jeans and pulled out an iPhone. "Which reminds me. I got you this. I put my number in there for you. I won't be around to protect you so much anymore. It's time for you to get with the times."

Jada took the slick piece of technology and held it awkwardly in her hand. Hopefully Ciara or Fleur would help her figure out how to use it. Because she was likely to break it on her own. "Thank you, but is this your polite way of telling me not to summon you anymore?"

Leon narrowed his eyes at her, but there was mirth there. "Yeah, don't do that."

Leon hugged her. He'd never done that before. But she may not see him again anytime soon, so she accepted it and relished the rare treat.

It didn't take long for everyone to prepare to leave.

The dragons decided there were too many in their party for them to carry and fly across the ocean especially since they didn't have any golds in their numbers to help them command the air.

Ciara, used her skills to talk their way onto the next over-booked commercial flight to Dubai, where Geshtianna's coven lived.

Dax paced up and down the aisles the entire time, grumping about how he hated to fly. Really, dragons on a plane was pretty funny, and Jada looked forward to telling Ky the story. Better than snakes on a plane.

There was no helping Dax, but Jada caught both Fleur and Ciara, one and then the other a few minutes later, take their mates into the lavatories for a little mile high club action. She didn't see how either of those guys even fit in that tiny room, much less how they'd engaged in sexy times. But, the two men did seem much more relaxed afterwards.

They arrived in Dubai at dusk, and although everyone had passports, it was easier for Jada to use her allure to get them all through immigrations faster.

It was at least a thousand degrees outside, which shouldn't bother Jada, but she'd gotten use to all things cool and icy, being around Ky. She was grateful Ciara arranged for the big black SUVs with the darkly tinted windows and superduper full-blast air conditioning.

Portia had been quiet the whole flight, and Jada had to prompt her for directions to wherever Geshtianna was staying.

Portia tapped in a text to someone and then gave directions to Jakob, who was driving. Turned out to be a high-end hotel, the kind where sheiks stayed. It wasn't five-star, oh no, it was a six-star hotel. Geshtianna had an entire floor.

Twin incubus and a succubus guards greeted them at the door to the coven's rooms. Greeted was a strong word for the meeting as neither said a word, but when they walked away, Portia followed, so the rest of them did too.

The incubus twin held up a hand at an ornate set of double doors, carved with old motifs and symbols, inlaid with jewels, and didn't let them pass.

"They're going in to see if Geshtianna will allow the dragons inside. I give you odds of about fifty- fifty." Portia fiddled with her phone.

Jada should ask for her number. They weren't family anymore, but she wouldn't mind knowing what happened to Portia after all of this.

She was about to ask, when her heart stuttered and she lost her balance. Jada reached for the wall to keep herself from faceplanting and sank to her knees.

"Jada, what's wrong?" Ciara and Fleur each grabbed one of her arms to steady her. They helped her turn and sit on the floor.

"I… I don't know. Something bad." Jada reached for the bone carving with Ky's soul shard inside. It had lost its buzz, the little life force of its own.

Ciara gasped and grabbed the soul shard on her own neck. "Jada, your shard. The glow is fading."

Jada glanced down, and her heart stopped beating altogether. No, no, no, no. She looked at the other two mates and they reflected back the fear she knew was written all over her face. "I can't feel him. I've known all this time that Ky was still alive. I didn't know how, but now that the feeling is gone. I'm completely empty."

The double doors to Geshtianna's inner sanctuary flew open. A tall lanky woman with long black hair stepped out. "I thought someone was playing a really bad joke on me. Dragons, here? What the hell do you want?"

Jakob, Steele, and Dax formed a wall between the women and Geshtianna. The succubus would have a powerful allure, and Jada did not want her to use it on these dragons. Mated or not, they would feel some of her compulsion. The fact that she wouldn't be able to completely control them would simply piss her off. That wouldn't help her find Ky any faster.

Jada struggled to her feet and slipped between Jakob and Steele. "We're here for my sister's mate."

Geshtianna's eyes flashed wide for a millisecond. "Well, this should be interesting."

She waved them into the room, mounted some steps on a raised platform, and plopped herself down into a chair with gold gilt and encrusted jewels.

"Stupid succubus." Geshtianna sat on her throne, looking as bored as a trophy wife, except for the flash of hatred she flashed at Portia. "I'm not sure what else we expected from half human."

"Where is Jett? I have the soul shard. I gave you everything you want. He and I can be together now."

This was a whole new side of Portia that Jada had never seen. There was fear in her voice, not the usual stone-cold apathy that Jada had mistaken for self-confidence.

Jada understood the desperation. She'd do everything she could to save Ky. But she'd learned something the coven had never taught her. Family didn't betray each other to get what they needed. The dragons were there for each other, no matter what.

What Portia had found was not love. This was something else twisted and dark.

Being the mate of someone who would ask her to screw over all the other important people in her life wasn't about love.

Geshtianna laughed, a sound more like sandpaper on fingernails on a chalkboard made of baby cries. She zeroed in on Jada.

"Your human need for love has blinded you. Leonard should've known better than to let your mother live, or you for that matter."

Portia stood on her toes and look all around the demons in this coven to find her mate.

Her sister may have betrayed her and Ky, and the dragon whose shard she had stolen, but she didn't deserve Tiana's rude bitchiness. Jada stepped up next to her sister. "Quit dicking us around. Where is my sister's mate?"

"Listen to the mouth on you. I bet all the boys like to hear your dirty talk, since I doubt they're attracted to your fat ass. How do you even feed yourself?"

All right, that was it. This bitch was going down.

A young man with dark black hair that hung in his face, and eyes like dark holes moved through the crowd and pushed Geshtianna aside. "I will take you to where the Blue Dragon Wyvern and the mermaid are being held."

Geshtianna grabbed for his arm, but he yanked it away. "No, don't be as stupid as these half-breeds. You'll ruin everything."

He turned on Geshtianna and pointed an inky talon at her, scales rippling across his neck and body.

He was the dragon they were looking for. A black dragon.

"Don't for one second think that I don't know how you and Dumuzid have been using me." The man's voice was a threat all on its own.

"Don't be ridiculous. I saved you. You would die down there in that hell if it weren't for me." Geshtianna's tone held as much malice as Jada had ever heard.

"I am grateful for that," he said, lowering his head in a half bow, "but you're not fooling anyone into thinking you did that out of the goodness of your absent heart."

Geshtianna scoffed. "Why would you help them? What did Dragonkind ever do for you but cast you aside?"

"I'm not doing it to help them. I'm doing it to defeat him." The words slipped out of his mouth as if he had practiced them a hundred times.

Jada whispered to Portia. "Him who?"

He must have a vendetta against a coven mate, or maybe another dragon who had claims to Portia too, or something.

Jett spun and turned those empty black eyes on her. "My father, Kur-Jara the Black Dragon."

*K*y fought the devil like a dog. They had both taken flight, and there wasn't exactly a lot of room in this cavern for evasive maneuvers. He slapped at chunks of rock on the ceiling, flinging them to either injure or get in the Black Dragon's way. The problem was that the Black Dragon hadn't been held in captivity with no food or water, whipped within an inch of death with a fire whip, or gotten sex advice from the First Dragon today.

Ky burned through the fury of Jada's betrayal pretty damn fast. Now he all he felt was an empty hollow core that did nothing for him.

He knew he needed to get back to plan A. Get Azynsa and get the fuck out of here. But with the Black Dragon directly on his tail, he needed a distraction to be able to escape.

Fallyn appeared at the entrance of one of the tunnels. She took one look around at the destruction, and ashy remnants of what were supposedly her kin, and laughed out loud.

Okay?

Ky would probably be off his rocker too if his birthday

present consisted of a couple hundred lashes of a fire whip every year.

The sound of her hilarity was just enough to get the Black Dragon's attention for a millisecond. Ky took advantage of that and flew straight at the asshole's underbelly, talons out. His scales protected him well, but all dragons knew each other's weakness.

The Black Dragon jerked up, to avoid Ky's attack, but instead it exposed the one area not completely covered in scales, right between his legs, the soft squishy place where he kept his cock.

Ky slashed and the Black Dragon rolled and roared in pain.

Too bad, no dick in his claws, but Ky had probably stopped the baby demon dragon-making machine for a while.

The Black Dragon crashed to the cavern floor and Ky went in the opposite direction, straight for Azynsa's prison cell. He considered snagging Fallyn and hauling her along with. No matter who or what she was, or why she was important to the Black Dragon, no one deserved the fate she had gotten.

Dammit, it might cost him to get her, but he had to try.

She was still laughing hysterically when Ky swooped down to nab her. He almost had her, but an enormous crash rattled the cavern like an earthquake.

Ky glanced around, the Black Dragon was back on his feet on the ground. Blood flowed from the wound between his legs. Even with his face twisted in hate and pain, he was also looking for the source of the crash.

A new flow of lava poured in from one side of the room and swimming along in the liquid hot rock, was Match.

Red Dragon Wyvern and master of fire and all things hot and melty.

About fucking time.

"Nice of you to join us, oh greatly late one."

Match assessed the situation in one glance and spit fire-balls toward the Black Dragon. *"Nice of you to get your ass captured."*

The Black Dragon howled, narrowly missing the first of Match's volley, but catching the rest of them on the ass as he took to flight and retreated down an opposite tunnel. A hard flick of his tail caved the tunnel in so that they couldn't follow.

Match growled and dug at the rockslide out, tossing some to the side and melting others with his fire. Of course, Match wasn't here to help Ky. It was red dragon vengeance that had brought him down.

Ky wondered if Match would even remember Azynsa.

Ky did. *"Match, leave it. He's likely caved that entire tunnel in. We need to get these women out of here. Now."*

Match wouldn't do a damn thing he didn't want to, but after one helluva day, Ky and wanted to go home. To Jada.

His heart skipped a beat. Jada. He did still want her. It wouldn't be an easy road ahead for the two of them, but he was not giving up on his mate.

Match gave a final blast to the tunnel and then stomped his way over to Ky. *"What women? I only know of one mermaid."*

"Yeah, there's a lot of weird shit down here. I don't get how you live in volcanoes." Ky moved to the side to reveal Fallyn behind him. He knew she was still there because she giggled for quite a while longer. She had quieted in the last few minutes though.

Match looked to where Ky indicated and instantly lost his shift. He shimmered back into human form and fell to one knee. "Fallyn."

His voice was barely more than a whisper.

Ky had never seen anything like this happen to Match. Even when he'd been contrite after challenging Ciara to prove that she was a true mate, he still had his alpha of alphas bravado. Nothing, no one shook him. What the hell had just happened? How could he know Fallyn?

Ky turned to see the girl's reaction. The smile immediately dropped from her face. There were no more giggles, the laughter was gone. Instead he saw only pure hatred, fueled by the fire in her eyes sparking like dynamite.

She pulled a dagger from a sheath strapped around her thigh and threw it toward Match. Her weapon narrowly missed Match's head and she grunted something angry that, Ky didn't understand in a harsh guttural language.

She threw another almost immediately after, which Match snagged straight out of the air.

She stomped her foot, turned, and ran up the tunnel.

"What the hell was that? Do you know her?"

Match examined the dagger in his hand and slipped it into his pocket. He didn't answer Ky's question, but shifted back into his dragon. *"You go after the mermaid, I'll find Fallyn."*

And then what? Match flew up the tunnel where Fallyn had disappeared.

"Guess I'll see you up top later, bro."

He was back exactly where he started, minus the Black Dragon.

Plan A. Get Azynsa, get the holy fucking hell out of this goddamn hellhole.

Ky headed up the tunnel where the prison cell cave was. *"Azynsa, ready to get out of here?"*

No reply. Shit.

At least he had his dragon back and could track her. Ky scented the air and thought for a second he caught a whiff of something sweet and fruity. Not likely down here. It was probably because he was starving and missed Jada. He would forever associate the scent of strawberry rhubarb with her badassness.

Thinking of her did several things to his body. He ached for her. Probably always would. But that ache came with a hollow gnaw, one that tried to warn him. He was going to get hurt. His age-old instincts told him to push that need for her away. Like a second serving of pudding,

He loved pudding.

Sometimes he ate it first.

And maybe that was the key to dealing with this problem of Jada. It wasn't like he was going to give her up, and he knew that even if their motives were working against each other, their bodies knew how to be together.

First, he had to find his way back to her. That meant finding Azynsa. The more he thought about it, the more he was sure who her mate was. But he would keep that information to himself until it mattered.

Azynsa smelled like the sea and old paperback books. Strange, but she was half human, so maybe she spent her time on land in a library.

He followed his nose through the winding tunnels, catching whiffs of other scents he was familiar with. Jakob, Ciara, Portia...and Jada.

Fuck, what was she doing down here?

What were any of them doing here?

He didn't want to think that Jada was working with Kur-Jara. Had she somehow used her allure to lure them to their dooms? She had already betrayed them all. Things may have escalated when the dragons figured that out.

She'd gone back to her coven. He knew she was closest

with Portia, and her father, Leon was a powerful old incubus. This would mean war between demons and dragons.

It hurt down to his soul to think that his mate could have been working against them all this time.

Ky needed someone to blame besides Jada, or himself.

The black rogue dragon. He must've brought them here. A little bit friend, mostly foe.

All of the scents intermingled at a junction of three tunnels. One was freshly hewn, and Ky recognized the work of the green dragon element of earth. They had dug their own tunnel down. Smart.

Had Jakob or Steele been coerced by the succubus allure, or did they think they were here on a rescue mission of their own? It must be the latter, because Jada hadn't been able to make any of the mated couples do her bidding.

Now he had an escape route. If Jada was really down here, screw the rest of them. He was getting her out of here. He would take her away where she couldn't hurt anyone else.

The group wasn't in the tunnel behind him, so he took the other one into the dark heat of the caldera as fast as he could. Their scents grew stronger, so he knew he was on the right path.

What would he find when he finally caught up to them? Would Jada pretend to be happy to see him? Now that he understood what her allure was made of, he could avoid it.

There were several smaller offshoots to this particular tunnel. Smelled like this was where the Black Dragon's army of demon dragons lived.

None of them were here. The supply of the little beasts seemed unending, but the dragon warriors had all battled and fought a great number recently. Maybe they had finally dwindled the demon dragon's numbers down.

Ky investigated several smaller rooms where Jada's scent was the strongest but didn't find any evidence of any of them until he heard a woman scream.

Jada.

Ky burst into the final room and found his band of not so merry men and women surrounded by an onslaught of demon dragons. Jakob was holding his own against them, supported by Ciara's use of the elements. She was throwing fireballs like a champ.

A black dragon stood in battle beside them. He wasn't as big as Kur-Jara in dragon form, but he was just as black. There was no mistaking: this was the rogue, the one the First Dragon had warned him about.

Jakob and the rogue had formed a triangle with Azynsa, pushing Portia, Ciara and Jada in the middle. Azynsa had her fists raised like a prizefighter, but Portia cowered. She was the one who had screamed. She did it again as a demon dragon tried to leap over the warriors to get to the gooey center.

Ky's eyes went directly to Jada. She looked up and met his gaze, grabbing the bone carving at her throat.

She had a look of relief on her face. There was no deception there, no lies wafting from her. He wanted to believe that.

Then she smiled at him, and the earth moved. Not literally, but in his heart. She was his mate. Always would be. Through good times and in bad.

He'd wait on those good times to come.

Time could have stood still for the two of them, but it wasn't that kind. Instead the world accelerated. Jada raised what looked like a tiny pink handgun over her head and shot at the nearest demon dragon. It fell and disintegrated.

That was no lady's Beretta. It was a fucking squirt gun filled with blessed rhubarb filling.

Badass.

The demon dragons had their backs to Ky, solely focused on the warriors in front of them. Big mistake. Huge.

A new energy renewed Ky, and he tore through the closest demon dragons like an orca, slicing and smashing a path to Jada. She did the same pulling more squirt guns from a bag in her hip as she emptied them. He was getting her a goddamn super soaker when they made it back to the surface.

When only a handful of the demon dragons remained, most of them split, retreating down the hallway Ky had just come up. Jakob, Ciara, and the black rogue finished the remaining ones off.

Jada dropped her final squirt gun to the ground and ran to him. She didn't give him a choice, she slid right up to him and under one of his wings.

"I thought you were dead. I can't feel you, in here I mean." She placed her hand over the bone carving that held his soul shard.

The one he had given to her, the one he'd been worried she didn't want.

Ky shifted into his human form and wrapped his arms around Jada. He couldn't help it. He had every intention of keeping her at arm's length until he could figure out why this wall of mistrust was between them, convince her to come away from the dark side. He'd even make her cookies.

The way she sniffled against his chest broke that vow to protect his heart. Her tears threw the new wall he'd built around himself on the floor and smashed it into a million little pieces.

He laid his cheek against the top of her head and held her tight for just a minute. They were still in the bowels of hell, but he needed this. They both did.

She hiccupped and sniffled again. "Why can't I feel you?"

Ky hadn't realized that the droplets of Azynsa's tears still surrounding his heart, his life force.

He released them with his thanks and pulled a few from Jada's face to replace them with. She gasped, and they both groaned as their connection was restored.

The blue shard of his soul glowed brightly again on her.

"Sorry, *wahine*. It got a bit rough down here for a while." He would tell her later about his meeting with the White Witch and the First Dragon.

Jakob cleared his throat. "Sorry to cut your reunion short, but I'd like to get out of here with my scales intact and my mate unharmed."

Ky was going to ask Jakob why he brought Ciara at all, but nah. She was a white witch, one who was still learning her powers, but from the day they had all first met her, nobody told her what to do. It drove Jakob crazy, which Ky found hilarious until very recently when his own mate had him questioning, love, life, and the meaning of everything.

The answer wasn't forty-two.

He had a million questions to ask her. It would be a difficult conversation. All of the whys would plague him if he didn't. He wanted to get on that path to forgiveness as soon as he could.

The way to do that was to get home.

"Match is down here too. Get this—he's chasing the Black Dragon's daughter." Ky looked over at the rogue. "You've got quite the family."

The black dragon shifted into his human form. He had no shard hanging around his neck, so Ky didn't understand how he was able to shift.

The rogue scowled at him. "They are not my family. I have no family."

Portia stood up and tried to take the rogue's hand. He pulled it away.

Ky noticed the shard hanging around Portia's neck right then. It was a dull yellow, but he would recognize it anywhere. It was Cage's.

Was that why Jada had stolen the shard? To give it to her sister?

Azynsa interrupted the spiral of questions that threatened to suck him under. "I'm not leaving yet."

The rogue turned on her and growled. "You need to get the fuck out of here. I've helped you as much as I could. But Kur-Jara will kill you if he doesn't get what he wants."

Azynsa lifted her chin. Such a defiant mate she was going to be. "I don't care. That woman, Fallyn, she made a huge sacrifice for me and was punished because of it. I have to find a way to repay her."

The rogue rolled his eyes. "Getting yourself killed will not help her. I'm not sure anything can."

"I have to try." Azynsa had such a look of determination on her face, they all knew they weren't leaving until they helped her rescue the Black Dragon's daughter.

The sooner they did that, the sooner Ky could get Jada back in his arms, back in his bed, back on his cock. Then he'd work on getting her back in his heart. "Then, let's find Match because he's on the hunt for her too."

MERMAIDS AND OTHER MATES

*J*ada had been overwhelmed with emotion when she first spotted Ky in the cavern. When he had opened himself up again and his life force rejoined hers she wanted very little more than to strip him naked and get it on with him right there on the floor of hell. But she'd held back because he had.

She understood he had almost died. That much she knew was true. But it didn't explain why he was acting distant now. There was something bigger wrong.

Was he mad that she had put herself in danger to come find him? How could she not?

Even now as they tromped through the flaming hot tunnels of this volcano he didn't look at her the way he used to. There was something he was holding back from her. A piece of himself.

Their relationship was pretty new, and she had spent most of it mistrusting him, but she would show him now that the worst was over.

She was his, fully. She wanted nothing more than for him to belong to her in the same way.

It was only fair of him to be wary. After all, Kur-Jara captured him because of her failed attempt to use her allure.

She hoped she wouldn't have to use it again.

Their little rescue party searched more tunnels than Jada knew existed in the world, with Ky using his tracking senses to lead them. Now was not the time for her to have any sort of conversation with him. But if it looked like things were going bad again, she wouldn't wait to make sure that he understood she was fully in. Not just in for the relationship, but in love.

She had told him the last time they were together, but it was in the throes of passion. People said a lot of things during sex. She'd heard it all. Lots and lots of declarations of love. She'd never returned a single one, until him.

She didn't want him to think that his skilled use of his fingers, tongue, and other sexy parts of him were the reason she had said those three little words.

Portia walked alongside of Jada, her head hanging low. This was one hell of a bed she'd made for herself. "Jada, do you think there's any chance that Jett and I will have what you and Ky do?"

Jada hadn't seen Jett and Portia interact all that much, but he continually pushed her away. In all of the other mated couples, including herself, the soul shards had been an integral part of the relationship. The one that Portia wore did not glow.

She had stolen it for Jett. But Jada didn't understand how that could work.

The soul shards contained a piece of each dragon's soul. Jett didn't have a soul shard. Did that mean he didn't have a soul? That must be what being a black dragon meant.

Maybe that was why both Jett and Kur-Jara were trying to take other dragons' soul shards. Perhaps, the Black Witch, Ereshkigal had a spell that would... what? Take these slivers of souls and transfer them to someone else?

The thought gave Jada a chill.

"I don't know. I only partially understand this dragon mating business, myself."

"Do you think that the mating is all that brought you and Ky together?"

Was it? Not a chance. The White Witch had intervened, but somehow Jada knew that she and Ky would have found their way to each other anyway. She didn't believe that love could be born from coercion, and that is what fate seemed like her. It may have thrown them together, but it was Jada's choice to love Ky. She hoped it was his as well.

"No. But it helped, as did the White Witch. Did she visit you too, is that how you knew Jett was your mate?" She didn't question Jett's lack of soul shard or how he didn't seem to actually like Portia all that much.

"I'm pretty sure I would have had a cow if I had met the White Witch. Are you saying you did?"

"Yes, although only briefly. Ciara and Fleur both did as well. She helped both of them find new power within themselves." Jada found herself a little jealous. But she was grateful that Ninsy had helped her.

"Geshtianna introduced me to Jett. She said she could tell that I was a dragon's mate. Jett is a dragon. The sex was phenomenal. Did you know that you can get a whole new level of energy from an orgasm? I wasn't even hungry for a week afterwards."

This was the girl talk Jada had wished she could have had

with Portia before she discovered the betrayal. "Yeah, I had that experience too."

Portia looked between Jada's face and Ky's back. "I bet you did."

Ky paused in front of them and then shouted, "Up ahead." He and Jakob rushed forward. Ky shifted back into his dragon form, but Jakob did not.

In a moment, Jada and the others saw why. Slumped against the side of an outcropping of rocks, sat a great big red dragon. His breathing was labored, a dagger was sticking straight out of the middle of his chest.

"Match, what happened?" Jakob examined the wound and Match's chest. The dagger didn't look that big, so it must have hit something vital.

Ky circled the small room. They were not in any immediate danger, because he shifted back to his human form too.

Match must have communicated something only to the other dragons. They exchanged a glance and then Ky pressed one hand against Match's chest and grabbed the dagger with the other.

Jakob knelt next to Ky and pointed at the knife. "On the count of three, you pull that out, and I will heal what I can. But I think it went directly into his heart."

Ky nodded and braced himself. Jakob blew a green mist over the place where the dagger stuck out of the red dragon's chest. Match groaned, and smoke rose out of his mouth and nostrils as he coughed at the pain.

"Now," Jakob yelled.

Ky pulled the dagger out and Jakob blew more green mist directly into the wound.

The red dragon shimmered and became a man again. "Be careful with that blade. Fallyn poisoned it."

"Bro. What did you do to that girl?"

Match did not respond.

"We need to get him out of here. That quick puff of healing dragon's breath won't be enough if the poison is still in his blood." Jakob helped Match to his feet and then supported him with his shoulder. "You're lucky to be alive, you son of a bitch."

"Where is she? Where did Fallyn go?" Azynsa asked.

Match shook his head. "I don't know. I just… She wanted to get away from me."

"I have to find her." Azynsa's voice trembled. She was so determined, but it sounded driven by fear.

Ky looked first at Azynsa and then over at Jada and Portia. "Azza, we can't leave you. You're a dragon's mate. And he needs you. He's dying."

Ky apparently knew who this girl's mate was. But how had it figured that out?

He waved Jada and Portia over to them. The shard at Portia's neck lost its dull color and began to glow.

"Ow, ow, ow." Portia ripped the shard from her neck. It had left a burn mark over her heart. "What is happening? Why did it do that?"

"It's as I suspected. That shard is not yours, and Jada never should have given it to you."

Umm, what? Pinpricks stung Jade's chest around her heart. This. This was why Ky was so standoffish. After everything, he still thought she was the thief who'd stolen Cage's shard.

Ouch.

She swallowed, and the pinpricks turned into the weight of a thousand stones on her chest.

Because she hadn't ever really let Ky get to know the real her. Had she ever let anyone see who she really was? She only barely knew herself. She never made real decisions, except what kind of ice cream to have that night. But whenever she and Ky were together he had openly trusted her. Had trusted that she knew her own mind.

He understood her better than anyone else, maybe even herself.

"I'm sorry, Ky."

Ky sighed and nodded. "I understand. I really do. She's your sister. I may be your mate, but it's only been a few days, and I swear to you I will do everything I can to make sure that in the future you can trust me."

Jada took his hand in hers and pressed it open palm to her chest, over the bone carving with his soul shard. "No, I'm not sorry about the shard. I didn't take it. I'm apologizing for is not giving you the chance to see the real me. I didn't give you any reason to trust me, so it's no wonder you think I betrayed you for my coven."

"I want to see you, Jada. I want nothing more than for you to let me in. I promise to keep you and your soul sacred."

"I know. I'm here. I can't promise that I will be perfect." Jada squeezed his hand tighter when Ky shook his head. "But I promise to keep you and your soul sacred too. You are mine, Ky Puru. And I am yours, fully, completely, and openly. Forever."

Blue light from underneath Ky's hand sparkled and filled the cavern. While everyone else stood watching, Jada and Ky's souls rose from their bodies in brilliant blue swirls and danced together, intermingling, becoming one. The new life in that act of magic settled on them like a warm rain. Ky grabbed Jada up in his arms and brought his mouth down to hers.

It didn't matter that they were standing in a literal hell, she was going to kiss this man of hers and savor him.

Their kiss was gentle but filled with so much passion. They tasted each other, lips brushing and dancing together just as the souls had.

Someone cleared their throat, actually several someones, and Jada reluctantly broke the kiss. She whispered against Ky's lips, "I love you."

"I know." He smiled and stole one more quick kiss. "I love you too."

Jakob cleared his throat. "Right, now that these two have made us all a little horny. Let's get out of here, so I can get my mate to spread her legs for me."

Ciara giggled. "Yeah, like you're gonna have to try really hard to make that happen."

Match groaned. "Great. Now we need another ring."

Portia still held the yellow soul shard, dangling it from its cord, so it didn't touch her. She looked at it with anger. "If I give this to one of you, will you return it to Cage? Tell him I'm sorry I fooled him into giving it to me. It's obviously intended for his true mate, and that's not me."

Jakob and Ky both moved to take the shard from her, but Jett stepped between them. "I'm sorry, Portia."

For the first time Jada thought she saw some emotion on Jett's face for Portia. But it wasn't love.

"What are you sorry for? It's not your fault that you don't have a soul shard of your own. Geshtianna told me that taking this one would make everything better."

Jett shook his head and frowned. "I'm sorry that you have been taken advantage of and led astray, and that I let that happen."

Portia's eyes went wide, and she stepped back. "What you mean?"

Jett's hand dropped to his side and he clenched his jaw. "Geshtianna is not a friend to either of us. She's lied to both you and me. But it's my fault for allowing the charade to go on so long. You are not my mate."

Portia wrapped her arms around herself, but the shard touched her skin and she yelped. She was on the verge of tears. She thrust her fist out and away from herself with the shard dangling as far from herself as she could get it. "Someone take this from me, now."

Jett grabbed her fist in his own hands. "No. It cannot go back to Cage now. Not once it has found his mate."

Both Ky and Jett's eyes turned to Azynsa. She took a deep breath and stood tall. She walked toward Portia, and with each step the shard grew brighter and its light illuminated scales on Azynsa's skin that Jada hadn't noticed before now. They were almost translucent, but in the glow from the shard's light they were a pearlescent gold.

Azynsa reached out for the shard.

"A shard can only be given, not taken. You must offer it to her, freely and willingly," Jett said.

Portia nodded, and took the two ends of the cord in either of her hands. "Here."

Azynsa bowed her head, and Portia tied the cord around her neck. The second the shard hit Azynsa's skin a golden light grabbed her body, lifting her into the air. It shot from her eyes, mouth, and fingertips, bowing her back. Her dark skin shimmered as the light settled all along it.

She slowly floated back to the ground. She looked around at each of them, a new light shining from her eyes, like sunshine had been captured in her irises. They were no longer brown, but shiny gold.

The surge of power receded to the spot where the shard lay between her breasts. Before any of the rest of them could even blink, Azynsa turned and disappeared into a tunnel.

The dragons moved to follow her, but Jett blocked their way. "She's gone. I don't know where, but she's no longer in those caverns and tunnels. I can feel every being down here and she's not one of them."

"You've got a lot of questions to answer, rogue. Including where that mermaid went. Let's go," Jakob said.

"Not this time, boys. Azynsa will be fine. I've got some havoc to wreak, and if you don't head back up your tunnel in the next couple of minutes, you're going to have a brand spanking new horde of demon dragons on your tail." Jett shifted into his dragon form and flew down the same tunnel Azynsa had disappeared into. A rumble and screeches echoed from inside.

Ky took a couple of steps into the tunnel and shouted over his shoulder. "I think he's holding the demon dragons back. Let's move, move, move."

Ky and Jakob shifted to their dragon forms. Ky stood at the tunnel's entrance and Jakob opened a fissure in the ceiling above them. Ciara lifted her hands and the onslaught of dirt and rocks fell to the side without hitting any of them.

Jakob picked up Match in his talons and nodded to Ciara. She grabbed Portia and the ground beneath them suddenly exploded, pushing Ciara and Portia up through the fissure.

"Ky, grab your mate."

Jada met him halfway, and he cradled her in his claws. They flew, twisting and turning through the ground for what seemed like forever. Jakob was right behind them with Match in tow. The ground closed up beneath them blocking any demon dragons from following.

They popped out of the earth into a wet and green oasis.

Dax, Steele, and Fleur were there waiting for them along with Ciara and Portia.

Fleur ran across the lush green grass and grabbed Jada up in a hug. "Ciara says we're planning another wedding."

They were?

Ky shifted into his human form again and chuckled. He pulled Jada away from Fleur, straight into the pool of water at the center of the oasis. "I don't think there's any getting around that, not with Ciara around. But I would like it."

The water and Ky's love washed over her, soothing her soul. She splashed little waves over both of them and then swam up to him, circling her arms around his neck and her thighs around his waist.

"I know what you would like, but are you asking me something?" She ground herself against him and found exactly what she was looking for. The water had revitalized him, and his cock pushed against the apex of her legs.

"Do you want me to ask you something, my curvy succubus?" He peeled the dusty shirt over her head and tossed it behind him into the water.

She did the same to him, but it took a little wriggling, which Ky didn't seem to mind at all.

"Geez, you two get a room," Match shouted.

When Jada glanced back, but she couldn't tell who he was actually speaking to since Jakob and Ciara were also wrapped up in each other. A thin layer of water rose from the edge of the pool and formed a dome over it, secluding Ky and Jada from the others.

"I still say we need to get that old grump laid. Now, where

were we?" Ky pushed his hands into her hair and pulled her in for a kiss. This one scorching. But he broke it way before she wanted him to. "I was asking you something, wasn't I?"

"Later, much, much later." Jada didn't want to wait any longer to be with Ky.

"No, I don't think so. I want to know the answer to this question before I make love to you."

"Yes. There's the answer to your question."

Ky laughed. "You didn't even let me ask."

"Is that the wrong answer?" She waggled her eyebrows at him letting him know it was time to get the show on the road because they both knew what they wanted from each other.

"I'm going to hold you to that. Because I have a lot of questions that yes might be the answer to."

"Well then, your first question better be can I take off your pants."

It was. They were both completely naked by the count of seven and back in each other's arms.

Ky licked over the blue dragon tattoo along Jada's collarbone. Hell, that felt good. She tipped her head to the side giving him more access. He bit her there gently, scraping his teeth across her skin. That sent a whiz bang whee ooh straight between her legs.

Ky's fingers followed that up with soft stroking starting at her dragon mark, down between her breasts, across her belly, and in between her legs. He found her clit already throbbing and hard.

She closed her eyes and basked in his touch, no longer afraid of what she thought she was supposed to do. Whatever they did together, felt right and felt good.

"Just remember, you said yes."

Ooh. That sounded promising.

GODDESS OF LOVE

Ky's need for Jada was stronger than it had ever been. Touching her and seeing her eyes fill with lust and love had him ready to explode.

She had a new air about her this time. A new confidence. And it was sexy as fuck.

While it was a turn on to dominate her, he didn't need it. All he needed was her.

He'd make her submit to him, any time she wanted. But all they both wanted now was to join, to be one again.

He made her come a dozen times. Mates liked that.

"Mmm, Ky. That feels so good. Don't stop."

She clung to his shoulders, her nails digging reflexively into him.

He loved this look on her face, like total comfort in herself and ecstasy combined. Even more, he loved that he was the one and only man to put that look there.

Jada moved her hips in time to the swirls of Ky's fingers around her clit. She no longer needed him to control her pleasure. She was taking it for herself.

Absolutely gorgeous.

"That's it baby. Take what you need. There's more where this came from."

She bit her lip and moaned as he increased the speed of his fingers through her wet folds. She closed her eyes and threw her head back. Those luscious pink nipples of hers puckered and he knew she was close already.

"Look at me, Jada. I want to see your eyes when you come."

"Ky, I...hell." She looked at him, her eyes glazed with pure sensuality. Her fangs had dropped and she licked her lips.

Oh, yeah. Her bite was deliciously erotic, but if she bit him now, he wouldn't last. There was no way he was coming anywhere but inside of her hot sweet cunt.

She breathed in heavy gasps and her hips thrust against him. He couldn't wait for when his cock was inside of her, and she rode him as hard as he did her.

"Ooh, Ky, I'm coming. I'm coming." Her words slurred into moans as her body shook and exploded for him.

Despite his vow to come inside of her, he was damn close to bursting himself, just from the glow of her sexual energy around him.

He floated her back into the water, letting its warmth embrace her. He needed a minute to cool down, because they were far from done.

"Ky," she sang his name. "I know you've got plans, but I want your cock inside of me, filling me. I need you."

How could he refuse? "I will fuck you anyway you want, *aroha*, but indulge me a little first. I've missed the taste of you."

"That's not fair. You can't make me decide between coming with your cock inside of me or your mouth on me."

"Sure, I can." Because eventually, she'd do both, and more. "Pick one, and then we'll do the other."

"Well, when you put it that way." She laughed.

He'd never heard her laugh during sex. She'd been so tied up in her head before.

This new place they'd found between them curled around his heart and squeezed in an embrace he never wanted to let go of him.

Jada hummed her pleasure. "I've been missing you tasting me too."

"That's what I like to hear." He pulled her over to him and guided her feet so she stood on the sandy floor of the pool. "Now, don't move. I'll be right back."

She gave him a funny look, definitely wondering where he was going. The answer to that was down.

Ky slipped under the water, letting his dragon do the breathing. He could stay under almost indefinitely because the water brought him the oxygen he needed.

He knelt before her, that beautiful pussy right in front of him for the taking. With the first long swipe of his tongue, her hands went into his hair and gripped his scalp.

Her plump thighs called out for him to tease them with love bites and scratches of his whiskers. She jumped at the first nibble and tried to direct his head back to her pussy.

He bit her again on the other thigh, watching the water tremor around her as she jumped. He soothed the nips with his tongue and then worked his way up her inner thigh to her sweet, sweet pussy.

It had only been a day and he'd missed the flavor of her like he'd been without it for a lifetime.

He swirled his tongue in circles over her clit. It was still sensitive from her last orgasm, and he took her gently.

Ky slipped deeper into the water and flipped himself

upside-down so her could slide his face all the way between her legs.

He lapped at her, dragging his tongue from her clit to her channel. Jada spread her legs wider, showing him she wanted this as much as he did. He thrust his tongue into her, fucking her.

Her muscles fluttered, all ready to come again. Ky wrapped his arms around her thighs and held her tight to his mouth, pushing his tongue in and out of her, loving the soft heat of her.

He called upon the water to push her farther and swirled a water eddy over her clit. Even through the dampening of effect of the pool between them, he heard her moan.

She was so turned on, so ready, the water washed away her juices, her body made more, preparing itself for him.

He elongated his reach with just the tiniest shift, pushing his tongue into the dragon form. He thrust it deeper inside of her and wiggle it back and forth along with the in and out motion.

That and the water swirling over her clit pushed her over the edge. Her pussy clenched and her thighs tightened around his head.

But, he didn't let up. He wanted another one from her. He pushed her, ate at her, fucking her with his tongue and the water until she shook again, trembling from head to toe.

He wondered if he could get one more out of her, but he didn't get to find out because Jada yanked him up out of the water by the hair.

"That better have been your tongue, mister, and not some sort of eel or something." Her face was flushed, and the grin on her face was a very satisfied one.

He flicked his dragon tongue at her.

"Holy cannolis," she laughed. "You had better patent, trademark, and market that move. I know a whole lot of incubi who'd pay top dollar to be able to do whatever you just did."

"I'm afraid that's an ancient dragon secret, and I think we'll keep that between us."

"Okay, but only if we keep it between us often."

"That, I promise."

Ky dragged Jada down into the water, forming a thin bubble of air around her body. He was a little worried it would freak her out, and at first, she was surprised, but once she looked around and saw the world that he did, she smiled at him.

By the First Dragon, he loved her and the way she trusted him. He would do everything he could to keep that trust from her every day.

They nestled into the soft sand, a layer of water cushioning her back. He guided her legs, one wrapping around his waist and the other over his shoulder.

His cock was hard and aching and only her body would satisfy the deep need he had for her.

He pushed through the bubble of air around her and into her pussy, just as wet, but hot and tight. In this position he could sink into her and he slowly inched in until he was balls deep.

Fuck, she'd taken all of him, and it felt so good, so perfect. She grabbed the back of his neck and pulled him in for a kiss. He thrust into her mouth and her pussy at the same time, each mimicking the other. They moved together, slowly at first, but soon the shard around her neck began to glow and their souls reached out to dance with each other again.

They became one, feeling each other's pleasure, each

touch, each tremor of nerve endings singing with the bliss of their joining.

Her pussy fluttered around his cock, driving them both closer to coming. She'd come enough already that her body reached for his but needed a push to reach that peak.

Ky guided Jada's hand between their bodies and her fingers to her clit. She used her own fingers to open herself wider and circle the little nub finding a rhythm in counterpoint to Ky's thrusts.

He split the water around their faces and looked at her eyes. They stared into each other's souls for what seemed like a beautiful eternity.

"Jada, *aroha*. Marry me." He struggled to get the words out of his mouth between heavy breaths. "I want the world to know how much I love you."

"Yes. I'll always say yes."

Yes. The best word in the world.

He wanted to see her face again as she came, but he needed to reaffirm his claim on her more. He bent his head to her shoulder and sunk his teeth into the curve where the dragon he'd marked her with shone against her pale skin.

Her body shook as he did. Jada twisted, and her mouth found his neck. She returned his bite with one of her own, taking his blood, and pushing them both over the edge into an explosion. They came together, wrapped in each other's bodies and hearts and souls.

Hours later when they were both sated, they returned to shore to find the other mated couples there. Match slept, but there was no sign of either Dax or Portia.

"They're not?" Jada asked.

"No," Steele said. He was friends with Dax and would have

known if the dragon and succubus were mates. "She asked him to take her back to the States."

"Speaking of states. Who wants to be in a wedded blissful one? Do I have three weddings to plan?" Ciara clapped her hands and gave both Jada and Fleur pointed looks.

"Jada did say yes." A whole bunch of times. Over and over and over.

"Squee. Ky, I've been studying up on the dance, what's it called, ooh, right, haka. There's one for weddings. Did you know?"

Ky couldn't help but smile at her enthusiasm. How long had she been planning his wedding, anyway?

"I did actually." He wrapped his arm around Jada and pulled her close, thinking about what Match had said in the tunnels about needing a ring.

Back before dragons had lost the ability to find mates, and the White Witch was still...alive, she bestowed a ring upon mates of Wyverns. Well, she made them find one.

If they found it, and could wear it, then they were worthy of being a true mate to a leader of dragons. Only the right woman could wear the ring for a Wyvern.

Ciara wore the last ring in known existence.

Damn.

Ky should have asked the White Witch for one when he'd seen her. Not that he'd been able to ask for anything at the time.

Ky didn't want to give Jada any old piece of jewelry; he wanted it to be special. Maybe Nana Kiki would have an idea for a ring.

In a week's time, Ky got to call his AllWyr in New Zealand. Cage had miraculously recovered. Almost. He was no longer knocking on *atua's* door. But he could no longer shift from man to dragon.

The one thing keeping Cage from going insane was the promise that he had a mate. Match made Cage a vow that as soon as he recovered from the stabbing and poison, together, they would descend back down into the earth and find Azynsa.

Match refused to even speak Fallyn's name, so they let him be. He wasn't that much different than his old grumpy self. While he recovered from the poison, he walked like a dragon in his Wisdom, nearing death, instead being in his Prime.

His brother Wyverns, along with Ciara and Fleur had all agreed to stand up at the wedding. Jada saved a spot in that line-up for Portia too. She had yet to reply to the request.

Ciara had wanted months to plan the wedding, but he and Jada insisted on a week at most. Ky was sure Ciara used her white magic to pull it all off.

The garden behind his house on the bay overlooked the ocean. His lands were filled with dragons, mostly blues who had swum in from all over the world to be at the first dragon wedding in their lives.

Many had already told him that seeing him with a mate had given them hope. They, like he, had never expected they would find one. Now it was a real possibility that they might.

The final detail nagging Ky was the ring for Jada.

It killed him that he couldn't find that for her. He'd searched his own treasure up and down and up again to see if there was any possibility a ring had been left behind. He found plenty of diamonds and jewels, but no ring.

He was sitting on the back terrace of the house, looking out over the water when Jada came and found him.

"Hey, Ky. Look what Nana Kiki and I found." The two

women walked out together arm in arm. Granted Nana Kiki was quite a bit slower than Jada and needed her cane to keep upright. She was at least a hundred years old, although no one knew her real age.

Nana smiled at Jada with so much affection in her eyes. They'd spent almost as much time together this week as Jada and Ky had.

"What is it, *aroha?*"

"Nana and I were digging around in some old boxes you have trying to find a dress she wanted to wear, and I found this."

Jada held out a ring, made of pure water. It swirled and sparkled, but held its shape, even as she laid it in his hand.

"She found that right away, she did," Nana said and sat in the chair opposite him, using her cane to help lower herself. "Why don't you put it on her finger, boy? I think it would look fine."

Ky's hands shook as he slipped the ring onto Jada's finger.

"Say the words, Kaiārahi. Jada, repeat after him."

"Ni, Jada," Ky paused. "I don't know your last name."

"Oh, uh. I don't really have one. I've always been identified by my coven. How about Leonardo?"

Ky nodded and smiled at her.

"*Ni*, Jada Leonardo, *cad men anna ni gud* Ky Puru."

Jada said the words back to him and a blue light as strong as the one in his soul poured from the ring, surrounding them both.

Ky said his vow back to her. "*Ni*, Ky Puru, *gud tammabuki, cad men anna ni ilati sinnis*, Jada Leonardo."

The light filled them both, and their souls danced again. As it faded, it gathered and sank into the water of Jada's ring.

Ky kissed Jada and held her tight to his chest. Then he looked over at Nana Kiki.

She had an awfully familiar gleam to her eye. She seemed younger. Was that a new white dress she was wearing?

"Ky, what were those words. What did we say? They felt familiar, right."

"They are the vows of the Wyvern mating ritual. You promised yourself to me and I to you."

"I love that. But, shouldn't we have said them tomorrow at the wedding?"

Nana Kiki rose, without the help of her cane. "Jada, your gift, what your offer is what every human wants, what every being in the universe is looking for, hoping for. What you offer is love. No one, mortal or not, can resist the allure of true love. Ky needed that in his life. He'd gone far too long without it."

"Nana? How did you know about the ring, and that I should put it on Jada? And the words? You were my father's companion. He had no mate."

She laughed and the air around her glowed. "While I enjoy you calling me Nana Kiki, it's not quite one of my true names. Although I have many. One is Inanna, another is Ki."

Holy First Dragon. Ki was a little-known name for *Papatūānuku*, the Māori primordial earth mother. The mother of all things.

A warmth washed over both Jada and Ky as Nana Kiki transformed before their eyes. She was a beautiful young woman. She was the White Witch.

"I should know, youngling." She kissed them both on the forehead. "I should know who your mates are. I'm working on that for your brothers now. Who better than me? I used to be the goddess of love."

In a blink, the White Witch disappeared, leaving Ky and Jada to gape in her wake.

They two of them told only Match, Cage, Jakob and Ciara about their ritual with the White Witch.

Each was floored by the story. Jada and Ciara compared rings. None of them had noticed that Ciara's was made of a literal living plant on her hand when Jakob had put it on her finger. But now that the mates of the green and a blue Wyverns had rings that matched their dragons' elements, they all looked forward to seeing what a ring made of sun and wind looked like for Cage's mate.

The wedding was a great party; his Wyr performed the *Tika Tonu* Haka for them.

It brought a tear to his eye to have his blues join in this ritual blessing he and Jada's new life together.

That evening, Ky took his bride to bed and they didn't come out for a week. Okay, ten days.

He loved her, not just with his body, but with his soul. She returned his love tenfold.

Never again would either of them have to hide their hearts away. In each other's arms and in each other's lives, they were living their true happily ever after.

KEEP READING with the next book in the Dragons Love Curves series - Cage Me.

NEED MORE curvy women getting their happy ever afters? Want to be the first to know when the next book comes out (plus get cool exclusive content from me!)? Sign up for my Curvy Connection mailing list.

You'll get book release news, contests and giveaways, and exclusive previews and excerpts. You can also join my review team for free books!

The Curvy Love Series

Curvy Diversion

Curvy Temptation

Curvy Persuasion

Curvy Domination (coming soon)

The Curvy Seduction Saga

Rebound

Rebellion

Reignite

Dragons Love Curves

Chase Me

Tease Me

Bite Me

Cage Me

Baby Me

Defy Me

More dragons coming soon!

Fated for Curves

A Curvy Girl Sci-fi Romance Series

A Touch of Fate

A Tangled Fate

A Twist of Fate

More Space Rangers coming soon!

WHO LOVES DRAGONS?

Dear reader,

I hope you loved reading this adventure in the Dragons Love Curves series with Jada and Ky as much as I loved writing it!

The dragons and their mates have a lot more adventures coming your way. So many questions to be answered.

Keep reading the Dragons Love Curves series to your fix of sexy dragon shifters giving their mates happy ever afters (and happy endings! Lol)

If you enjoyed this book in this series, check out where the story began in Chase Me, Ciara and Jakob's story.

The next full-length novel in the series is, Cage Me. You'll get to read about Cage Gylden, the Gold Dragon Wyvern and his mate, who might happen to be a mermaid.

A fish and a bird can fall in love, but where would they live?

Keep turning the pages for a preview of Cage Me just to wet your whistle on their story.

I'd love to hear what's on your dirty little minds, so be sure to leave a review for this story. I really appreciate you telling other readers what you thought.

Need more curvy women getting their happy ever afters? Want to be the first to know when the next book comes out (plus get cool exclusive content from me!)? Sign up for my Curvy Connection mailing list.

You'll get book release news, contests and giveaways, and exclusive previews and excerpts. You can also join my review team for free books!

Find me at www.AidyAward.com or on Facebook, Twitter, Instagram, or follow me on BookBub.

Kisses,

~Aidy

A flying dragon and a mermaid can fall in love, but first he has to convince her to return from hell.

Cage Gylden is one lucky son of a dragon. He should have died when his soul shard was stolen, but his mate saved his life.
Too bad he's never met her...and she's in hell.
As a warrior he will do everything in his power to defeat the Black Dragon and rescue her, whether she wants to be saved or not, even if he has to sacrifice his own life.

Everyone Azynsa loves gets hurt... or dies. She won't allow herself to feel for those around her, not since her police officer father died and her mother's people, the Mami Wata mermaids came for her. But, she will not allow anyone else to sacrifice for her, ever again.
Fated mates or not, these two are in for one hell of a time trying to save each other, and themselves.

NEVER SAY DIE

He would not quit.

He would not let his people down, nor his mate. The warrior inside of him would never allow it.

Cage threw a punch, ducked and weaved, then threw another. He might not be able to shift into his dragon form anymore, but he could still fight.

He growled at his opponent who treated him like a little fucking flower. "Come on, Zon. Bring it. Don't go easy on me. My bare knuckles are all I've got left to fight with. I'm not quitting until they're bruised and bloody."

If he had to die trying, he would ensure the future of the gold dragons.

His sparring partner lunged and caught Cage right on the jaw, snapping his head back. He tumbled to the floor and spit out the blood pooling in his mouth. Served him right for navel-gazing. Warriors didn't think, they didn't screw around.

About time he learned that lesson.

Better late than never.

Probably.

"Sorry, sir." Zon looked down, the telltale worry in eyes. God, how Cage was tired of concerned looks. He'd lost his dragon, but it didn't make him a breakable baby.

He waved the offered hand away. "I'm fine. But remind me to dock your pay later."

That anxious look turned to shock. Thank the First Dragon, because one more second of being pitied and Cage really would start docking warriors' pay.

That would teach them. Gold dragon warriors were greedy bastards.

"Kidding, man. Teach me that move and I just might give you the key to my lair."

Another look of shock. Cage really needed to get his men to lighten up.

Worry was not the way to be a warrior. Action was.

AmberGris, his second in command, and Zon's twin walked into the training room and frowned at Cage lying on the floor. He assessed the situation, folded his arms, not pleased, and scowled at Zon, who shrugged.

The two exchanged glances that had a whole lot of – what the hell is going on here – I don't know, he asked me to spar with him – well, you have to be careful with him, he's weak – communication between them. Before Cage could smack them both upside the head, Gris gave him the news he'd been waiting for.

"Sir, we have her."

Cage ignored everything else and pulled himself up from the mats. "Good work. Put her in my office and draw the shades. We want to make our guest is as comfortable as possible."

"Respectfully, sir, she's been a giant pain in the ass and I would prefer we escort her to the dungeon where I – we - can keep a better eye on her."

Gris was an excellent dragon warrior... and a little overdramatic. Cage had turned The Lindens' dungeon into a wine cellar years ago. But, since this whole shit storm had started, Gris had become an overprotective mother hen.

"I'm sure you would. Put her in my office anyway."

Gris grumbled, and Cage could practically see his feathers puffing up. "Sir."

Cage raised up a hand to hold the oncoming objections. "I promise you and the rest of the guard won't be far away when I question her. She's already stolen my soul shard once. It's not like she can get it again."

Cage waved to his empty chest. It still felt strange to not be wearing the talisman that held a piece of his soul intermingled with the First Dragon's.

She'd stolen a whole hell of a lot more from him than his shard, shc'd taken something precious from every Golden Dragon.

And it was his own damn fault.

Gris huffed and puffed, stirring up small dust devils, but went back to his duties. Probably going to put about twenty more dragons on patrol around the little succubus.

Cage couldn't blame him, and if worse came to really fucking worst, Gris would make a good Wyvern. Not that he wanted the job, but if Cage didn't accomplish this mission, well, let's just say he'd plan the coup himself.

There is only one way Cage could be the true Wyvern his golds needed. That was to get his dragon back. There was only one way to do that.

Go to hell and find his mate.

There was a lot more riding on Cage finding his mate than

just his own forsaken soul. The souls of the rest of his Wyr and all their potential mates depended on it.

No pressure.

Jakob and Ky, Wyverns of two of the other dragon Wyrs had already found their mates. The first in centuries. None of them had even thought it was a possibility.

Since then, in just a few short weeks, at least a dozen more dragons had found, marked, claimed, and mated women who filled their souls and their powers to overflowing. But, only Jakob's greens and Ky's blue dragons had been blessed.

The reds and his own golds were just fucked.

The AllWyr council had surmised that the Wyvern of each Wyr must have to be mated before the rest of his dragons would be able to.

The only thing keeping Cage from going berserk and killing every demon dragon under the sun was the fact that he already knew who she was.

Azynsa.

Such a strange and beautiful name.

It was almost all he knew about her. That and she was half mermaid.

The fates had to be laughing their asses off for coming up with that one. A flyer of the skies and a lush creature of the ocean, soul mates.

Where in the world would they live?

He'd figure that out later, assuming they both survived long enough to get together.

Azynsa already owned his soul.

Quite literally.

He'd known it the instant she'd touched his missing soul shard. She'd healed him from the worst case of man-flu in the universe. Even though they'd been on different planes, separated by miles, space, and time., he knew her and their connection.

Weirdest fucking feeling ever. Like a miracle wrapped up in an enigma sprinkled with fear and fairy dust.

Azynsa was his true mate, and he was hers.

Only problem, she'd been kidnapped by the Black Dragon, the king of hell, and when his brother Wyverns had tried to save her, she'd… disappeared.

Ky and Jakob had left her on the promise from some shit-head of a rogue dragon, that she too had escaped.

He knew better.

She was down there. Tortured by the heat and something that weighed heavy on her heart. He'd had dreams of her hiding, spying, crying.

No, not crying. She had yet to shed a tear.

The dreams were not his imagination. He suffered her pain and sorrow as if he were there with her. A part of him was.

He'd also known her bravery, an internal toughness that even most dragon warriors couldn't match.

She was one badass mermaid.

Every waking hour he plotted and planned, trained his human body to fight and survive, all so he could rescue her from the pits of hell.

He had a strategy to get a guide to hell. Once he got down there he'd have to survive without his dragon in a realm filled with demons, demon dragons, the Black Dragon, and no possibility of sunshine, to recharge him, ever.

None of the dangers mattered, not if they meant he could rescue Azynsa and lift whatever spell was keeping his Wyr from finding their mates.

Cage headed to the main house and stretched out while

crossing the garden, basking in the direct rays of the sun. He really ought to live on a beach somewhere, but Denmark and The Lindens estate had been the Gold Wyr seat for longer than he could remember. Besides, a big chunk of his treasure hoard was here. It would be a giant pain to move, and how did one hide billions of dollars of gold, art, gold, jewels, and more gold in the sand?

He got plenty of sunshine here and when the skies were gray and cloudy, all he had to do was fly above them to refill his energy.

Except he couldn't do that anymore.

He couldn't live without the sun and not just because he needed to work on his tan. Which meant hell…would be hell.

He was going there anyway.

He'd already decided not to ask Jakob or Ky to join this battle. It wasn't fair to them or their new mates to ask them to put themselves at risk again. Match was the perfect choice to go with, that bastard loved the dark and heat of a volcano. But, he was still recovering from a dagger to the heart, poisoned with something that had almost killed him.

He'd be grumpy the whole time anyway. He was always grumpy.

Time to get creative.

Actually, he already had.

He closed his eyes and lifted his face to the sun, for one more minute of its energy. He had a feeling he would need all he could get.

When he got back to the house, two of his gold warriors were standing guard at the entrance to his office.

Behind the closed doors someone swore like a sailor who was raised by swearing sailors.

He'd always had a thing for filthy mouths.

"You two can go. I don't think you need to hear this."

They nodded and saluted and then stood there like statues. They weren't going anywhere. None of his guard had let him alone for a month. Either that or the succubus allure had them constrained.

He scowled at them and they didn't even flinch.

Fine, it was their dicks.

He pushed through the door and it took his eyes a minute to adjust to the dark room. All of the curtains had been drawn and the lights were off.

"Don't you come a fucking step closer to me, Cage. I have no intention of dying today."

Cage found his little thief stuffed into the corner of the room, hiding behind his desk. She had a letter opener in her hand, ready to use like a knife. There was a lot of bravado in her words, but the tremor behind them betrayed her fear.

She should be afraid.

"Hello, Portia. Stole any other souls lately?"

He knew full well she hadn't done anything besides run for the past few weeks. She'd been excommunicated from every demon coven in the world. She had to be scared, lonely, and hungry. Exactly how he wanted her.

"Screw you, you gave it to me."

That tough exterior had been what attracted him to her in the first place. That and her allure. Which she wasn't using now. Interesting. Cage's eyes adjusted to the dark and he sauntered toward Portia. "We've already done the screwing part, my dear."

She held the letter opener at the ready, and she knew how to wield it too. Leonard had taught her to fight. It was probably the only reason she was still alive. Succubae did not do well on their own.

"I'm not apologizing for all that. I did what I thought I had to do."

He wasn't blaming her, never had. It was his own damn fault for getting involved with a succubus in the first place. Well, it was his dick's fault.

He liked sex just as much as the next dragon, maybe more. Who better at sex than a succubus?

But truth be told, he hadn't been that into it lately. He figured it was just his Prime coming on. Dragons from his generation and the one before him, were well known to be horny little fucks in their younger days, but when they hit around a hundred and fifty and their aging slowed down, so did their libidos. He wasn't really ready to throw in the towel, like Match had.

That guy needed to get laid more than anyone he knew.

Cage's latest partners hadn't been disappointed. He knew how to make a woman come, screaming his name. He hadn't got off himself in months.

Portia's allure had gotten a rise out of him though. She'd worked her mojo and he'd welcomed it, with open pants.

He'd been so under her spell, that she could have asked for the moon, and he would've flown up to give it to her. But all she asked him for was his soul shard.

Even while he handed it over to her he knew it was a horrible idea. But, she'd controlled him completely.

Not today.

Cage flipped on the light switch, keeping her as off balance as he could. She preferred the dark.

He preferred to have a soul.

She squeaked and dove under the desk.

"I'm not here to eat you, Portia." Although she probably would've liked it. "I'm calling in the favor you owe me."

"I don't owe you shit." Her voice came up from her hiding place.

Cage laughed darkly. That was the most hilarious and horrible thing he'd ever heard. "Oh, I think you do. You owe me a whole lot more than that. But, I've got a deal for you. Do what I ask, and I have something for you in return."

He kept his tone seductive, doing his best to speak her language. Portia and what was inside her head were his best and only plan to get to hell and back.

"If that something involves chopping off my head, I'll pass, and also, fuck you."

"I hear you're homeless, without a coven. Not a friend in the world. Wouldn't it be nice to have someone on your side again, Portia?"

She gripped the edge of the desk and her face slowly rose above it. "What are you offering?"

Gotcha.

"You help me find my mate, and you can live here, under my protection. We'll find a way to feed you in any way you might need."

It wouldn't take much of her allure to get most of his dragons to fuck and feed her. Except maybe Gris. He had a particular hard-on for Portia, and not the fun kind.

Portia's face went paler than usual and sunk back down below eye level of the desk. "Why would you do that for me?"

Cage leaned against the desk and crossed one leg over the other as if none of this mattered to him one bit. "You have the key to getting me down to hell."

"Oh no. I'm not going back there."

He needed to entice her a little bit more. "I can provide you with everything your coven ever did and more."

"I doubt that. Leonard and Geshtianna are very old

demons. They're a lot more powerful than you or any of your dragon buddies."

Yes, but he had a trump card. "Maybe, but I can give you something they can't."

Portia was playing tough, but Cage knew he had her hooked. Her incubus father was powerful, but he'd also banished her. She had nothing, and he was about to offer her everything.

Cage waited patiently for her mind to come to the conclusion all on her own that she had no other choice. Regardless of what he was he had for her, it was a better option than life on her own. She knew it and so did he.

He could throw her in the dungeon and feed her on rats and she'd take it. Lucky for her he was offering something much better.

"What do you want from me? I can't take you down there. I was just along for the ride and lost everything while your dragons were off saving the day. Go ask them to help you."

"They've done enough. Besides, they don't have what you do." He had no intention of taking Portia back down into hell. She wouldn't be able to help him. Only one dragon could do that.

"Quit dicking me around and tell me what you want. My allure might not work on you or your golden retriever, but I'm pretty sure those two at the door are ready to come in here and fight you for me."

This sparring was the most fun he'd had in weeks. At least Portia didn't treat him like everyone else in his life at the moment. They were both vulnerable and that put them on an equal footing. "Why is it you haven't just turned your allure on me again? We both know you could simply make me tell you my plans and take whatever you want in the process."

"Yeah, like I haven't tried?"

He hadn't felt a thing.

Portia sighed. "Jada says our allure doesn't work on dragons who are mated, you bastard."

That may be true, but it wasn't why she didn't have any power over him. If he was mated, then the rest of his dragons would be finding their mates too. He was in a weird half-mated limbo.

She hadn't been able to dissuade Gris from his task of capturing her either. Her allure must be on the fritz from not having fed. The human side of her was probably the only thing keeping her alive.

Once their deal was done he'd have Gris bring her a nice big meal of human food. If she wanted or needed more than that, he'd feed her himself if he had to. But, only blood this time.

Cage had drawn this game out with Portia long enough. She was desperate already, but now that he'd dangled a safe future in front of her, she'd be ready to give him the one person he needed, betrayal or not.

"I've got the money and resources to give you everything you need. All you have to do is help me with one thing."

"Like I have a choice?"

"We always have choices, babe. We don't always make the smart ones though. I'm proof of that, aren't I?"

Portia crawled out from under the desk and stood, the letter opener still gripped in her hand, but finally she faced him. "What do you want?"

"Your boyfriend."

She frowned and held out the letter opener. "Fuck off. Jett's not mine to give. Never was."

Yeah, and that black dragon bastard never should have let

her think otherwise. But he had started this and Cage was going to finish it. "But, you'll find a way to get him here and get him to do what I want anyway."

She bit her lip and shook her head. "I don't know if I can."

"You'll find a way, because once he and I retrieve my mate," that was the plan, "you'll get yours."

She backed away. "Get my what?"

"Your mate, Portia." Boom.

"I don't think it was a coincidence you came to me to get a soul shard. Your mate is a gold dragon. Once I claim Azynsa, your mate will be able to claim you."

Portia dropped down into the chair, shock and awe on her face. Cage knew the feeling.

"Jett is going to kill me for this."

Not if Cage got to kill Jett first. But only after they went to hell and back.

———

Click here to get your copy of Cage Me now!

ABOUT THE AUTHOR

Aidy Award is a curvy girl who kind of has a thing for stormtroopers. She's also the author of the popular Curvy Love series and the hot new Dragons Love Curves series. She writes curvy girl erotic romance, about real love, and dirty fun, with happy ever afters because every woman deserves great sex and even better romance, no matter her size, shape, or what the scale says.

Read the delicious tales of hot heroes and curvy heroines come to life under the covers and between the pages of Aidy's books. Then let her know because she really does want to hear from her readers.

Connect with Aidy on her website. www.AidyAward.com get her Curvy Connection, and join her Facebook Group - Aidy's Amazeballs.

Made in the
USA
Columbia, SC